SEDUCTION OF A DUKE

JR SALISBURY

OLIVER HEBER BOOKS

Cover Design by Wicked Smart Designs

Published by Oliver-Heber Books

0 9 8 7 6 5 4 3 2 1

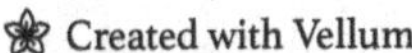 Created with Vellum

1

Lady Cora Keats rose, alongside her father, the Duke of Dover. Together they eagerly watched his racehorse, St. Elmo's Fire, take the lead. He roared past his competition with ease, as his magnificent, well-muscled back form carried him ahead by four lengths. Gentlemen began to shout, even though the race was far from over. Cora's enthusiasm was addictive. Thoroughbred horses were in her blood. For her, it wasn't just about the possibility of winning. To Cora winning was secondary. It was all about these magnificent creatures, watching them blossom from wobbly foals to training and on to racing.

Leaving her father's side and making her way to the rail, she stood at the edge. As she leaned forward over the rail, a large, flashy chestnut began to challenge her stallion. Oh, hell no! This would never do. Whoever this was, he'd better have stamina, because her horse had racing in his blood, with the endurance and speed of three horses.

She began shouting. "Come on! Come on! Move your bloody arse!"

Not one to lose, St. Elmo's Fire made his way to the

finish line in a second burst of speed, leaving the chestnut several lengths behind.

Smiling she turned to find her father watching her from the edge of the box, a stern look on his face. Her gaze turned back to the rest of the boxes and found a gentleman with wavy dark hair, the color of ink, watching her. His skin appeared bronzed from the sun. Too bad he wasn't closer so she could get a better look at him.

She loved the track at Sandown Park. Located in Surrey, it was an easy ride from their London home. The course itself was fast, and if she ever had a hunter ready for racing, this was the perfect course to start one on.

Cora got so absorbed in the race she forgot herself and who her father was. Words would fly from her mouth that she normally only used at the farm in Scotland.

Lanarkshire was located not far from Edinburgh in the Scottish Lowlands. The castle, appropriately named Keats Castle, had been in the family for over four hundred years. It was where Cora had spent most of her childhood, and where she fell in love with horses. At the tender age of four, she was given her first pony. From there, she was a constant figure in the stables. If she wasn't riding, she was asking questions of the grooms or stable master.

Her first racer had been a hunter named Lancelot. A white thoroughbred, he was quick and nimble, especially going over the walls and fences throughout the estate. By then, her father indulged her when she approached him at age fifteen about training a three-year-old piebald named Warrior, omitting the small fact that she was going to train him to race and hunt. Her dream was becoming a reality.

She'd always known what she wanted. She was confident, self-assured, and at times outspoken, never believing in keeping her opinions to herself. The majority of her time was spent in the stables, where she trained flat racers, and as St. Elmo's Fire's victory proved, she was quite good at it.

Her mother's death from a respiratory disease struck Cora especially hard; grief had overwhelmed her. She and her mother had been extremely close. Her death left her feeling empty and alone. Her passion for horses became her life. A way to escape her grief. Cora merged herself further into her horses. She would honor her mother by being the best at whatever she set her mind to.

Now here she was, not so very many years later, being escorted by her father to the winner's area once again.

~

"MOVE YOUR ARSE! Move your bloody arse!"

Sebastian Steele, Duke of Hightower, watched in fascination at the young woman standing at the rail yelling and making a fool of herself. Fascinated, because he'd never seen a woman get so animated about a horserace. It was undignified, and certainly unbecoming of a lady. Where was her husband?

Though women did attend horse races with their husbands, they never behaved like this. She appeared to be a peer, well dressed and mannered, except for this outburst. Could it be her husband's horse she was carrying on about?

She continued watching the race, cheering them on. In the sun, red hues sparkled off her mahogany hair. She wore a dark green dress with charcoal piping, along with a peplum jacket and skirt. The collar hugged her chin and was trimmed with black lace. The jacket closed with small black buttons on the front.

He turned his attention from the dark-haired woman to the race, which was winding down. The horses were headed into the homestretch, and his own entry, Apollo's Gold, was proving once again to be a disappointment, holding at a good distance behind the winner. The stallion had shown great promise up until the last two races. Something was missing. He needed to send Apollo to someone who could salvage this horse's future before he ruined it.

"Better luck next time," Crispin Allgood, Earl of Yorkshire said, clapping him on the shoulder.

"There isn't going to be a next time, if I don't figure out what's holding him back," Hightower grumbled.

"Perhaps you need a new rider."

"I switched riders the last race and the results were no better. Something else is going on."

"Have you ever considered sending him off for training? Perhaps he needs a fresh pair of eyes guiding him. You're too close, Hightower. You've raised him from an orphaned colt. I understand the Duke of Dover uses one of his estates in Scotland exclusively for training and breeding. His trainer is supposed to be excellent. You saw the result just now."

Hightower jerked his head to the rail. She was gone. He turned back to Allgood. "Who's his trainer, do you know?"

"I can't recall offhand. Just heard he runs the Duke's entire operation there, and like I said, the man's excellent," Allgood replied.

"I need to make inquiries."

"Indeed. Are we off to town, or do you want to go to the stables first?"

"Stables. Make sure Apollo is readied for the trip home. I think a week or two running the meadow might help his state of mind while I contact Dover's trainer, don't you think?"

"I agree. After, perhaps we can make our way to White's for a drink and an early dinner."

"I certainly could use a good snifter of brandy after this disappointment," Hightower said.

Hightower's own stable was relatively small. With three generations of Irish Thoroughbreds, some crossed with Arabians, his breeding lineage was becoming known.

Apollo's Gold had been orphaned at birth, his mother dying shortly after having him. Hightower had personally taken an interest in maintaining the colt's feeding schedule at night, allowing the stable boys some much-needed time off. Many nights, Hightower slept in the colt's stall.

Now a three-year-old, the flashy chestnut colt had proven he had what it took to race like the wind. Until two races prior. Despite all the small changes with riders and feed, nothing changed. Apollo's Gold seemed more lethargic and uninterested. He merely went through the motions. If Hightower couldn't figure out what was going on with the colt, he would have to retire him from racing and find another use for him. Or worse yet, find another owner, though Hightower knew he could never part with the chestnut. He'd made him a promise that first night, as he fed the youngster in his stall, that they'd always be together.

Before making any decisions, he would look into sending him off for further training. His friend was right. Though the youngster had the heart of a racer, Crispin was right, he was too close to the colt.

It was said the Duke's farm employed a most unusual and competent trainer, who had led the Duke's horses to victory on the track. The trainer was also known to know horseflesh and breeding better than most, which could prove interesting. Perhaps he might learn something new from this man. Tomorrow he would make inquiries and see about visiting the Duke of Dover's training farm in Scotland.

They climbed into Allgood's carriage, heading for White's. "You said you couldn't tell me much about the Duke's trainer. Tell me what you have heard."

"Only that he's done remarkable things over the years improving the Duke's bloodline. So much so, I hear the Duke sold a young colt to some European royalty recently for an obscene amount of money. 'G.S.' I believe is what the fellow goes by. Not sure about a surname, but it'll come to me."

"I think I'll contact the Duke and make an inquiry about training."

"Excellent idea because they might not be accepting outside horses right now. You might have to be scheduled."

"Precisely. Perhaps I can temp the Duke to meet me at the farm and introduce me personally to his trainer. Do you know where it's located?"

Allgood smiled. "It's located in Lanarkshire. In the Scottish Lowlands. I do not have the interest you do in horses and racing and such. I'm sure you can find out easily enough. Simply make some inquiries. Tattersall's might be a good place to start. I understand some of the Duke's lesser quality horses go through there."

"It sounds like Dover keeps everything rather exclusive and quiet."

The carriage came to a stop in front of White's. A footman opened the door to let them descend the carriage. Hightower followed his friend. His interest was even more piqued now.

"Do you have any plans for the evening?" Allgood asked.

"Nothing that can't wait. Why?"

A footman appeared and took their drink order after they sat down in a couple of leather chairs off to one side. Hightower ordered whiskey and the Earl did the same.

"I thought we might have steak here and then proceed on to The Tortoise and Hare," Allgood smiled. The Tortoise and Hare was a supposed gentlemen's club. One that discreetly offered their clientele women to satisfy their needs when a wife or lover could not.

"Hyacinth not at home?" Hightower asked with a smirk.

"No. She's visiting her sister in Manchester. She won't be home for another fortnight."

"Really?"

Allgood nodded. "Her sister is with child and is about to give birth. It's her first, and Hyacinth thought she should be there for the blessed event."

Hightower took the glass from the footman who'd returned with their drinks. "You really need to get yourself a mistress rather than frequenting gentlemen's clubs."

"Says the man who is celibate."

"I've just not found a woman worth keeping as a mistress. As far as your question about this evening? I'm afraid I'm going to have to pass. Not to my taste."

"What has gotten into you, Hightower? You've gotten to be quite boring, you know." His friend grinned and upended his drink.

Knowing his friend's fondness of whiskey and brandy, Hightower motioned for a footman and ordered two steaks, along with more drinks. He didn't need to accompany Crispin tonight. The last time he did, it took him a week to recover fully.

If it hadn't been a marriage arranged by both families, Hightower was sure his friend would have never married. At least not yet. Crispin enjoyed whoring around far too much. Which was why he had no mistress. A mistress would be too confining, and he had a wife for that.

A couple of hours later, after drinks, dinner, and brandy afterwards, Hightower called it a night. He left his friend at his carriage and found a hansom to take him home. He wanted to see how the colt fared. He had been brought to the mews behind his London home rather than make the trip back to the estate, as Hightower was thinking a good night's rest was more of what Apollo needed.

The streets were busy in this section of Westminster. Carriages lined the street, taking their occupants to the theater or social affairs. He was thankful to be on his way home, though his country estate was more to his liking. Coming to Town was a necessary evil, and he would just push through it.

As long as he limited the social engagements he attended, the more likely he might be left in peace. The only way he saw he could avoid the anxious mothers wanting to make sure their daughters got an introduction with him, or better yet, that he would dance with one of them.

He knew he needed to marry at some point, start a family, and produce the next Duke of Hightower. But he would not be forced by his sisters or anyone else into marrying. Marriage would be on his own terms.

Beatrice, Theodora, and Matilda were all still single, and all were of marriageable age. What he needed to be doing was seeing they were married first. Then he would put himself out on the marriage mart.

He arrived back home, met by his butler, James, who took his hat, gloves, and greatcoat. He went down the hall to the library. A book about the Roman empire sat where he'd left it the night before. The book was dry reading, but his fascination with ancient civilizations held his attention, letting him immerse himself in some long-forgotten battle.

Pouring a brandy, he settled onto one of the settees his mother had furnished the room with years ago. He took a thoughtful sip of the dark amber liquid before opening the book to where he'd marked it the night before. After reading and rereading the third page, Sebastian picked up the brandy and finished it off, not understanding why he was unable to focus.

His mind kept going back to Apollo and the astounding loss the colt suffered earlier. Beyond that, he recalled the dark-haired beauty yelling at the rail. As enthusiastic as she was, he wondered if the horse belonged to her father or husband. The only other reason for her acting in such an unladylike fashion would be that she'd simply bet on the horse and had gotten carried away as the colt blew past all the others, winning by at least a half-dozen lengths. Apollo could do that easily. He was more than capable to outrun every horse he'd been against today. He just failed to deliver. Something was terribly wrong, and somehow, by hook or by crook, Sebastian was going to figure it out.

2

Hightower pulled the covers up over his head as the heavy forest green draperies opened, revealing a bright, sunny morning. Damn Titus—the majordomo knew not to wake him before eight unless it was an emergency. An emergency constituted the house on fire or some other dire and dreadful disaster. Anything else could wait until he awoke, dressed, read the newspapers, and took a light breakfast.

"Good God, man! This had better be good!"

"I can assure you it is," Allgood replied, a mocking tone to his voice. "Besides, you're wasting a perfectly good day lying about in bed.

Knowing he'd get no peace from his friend, Hightower reluctantly sat up and swung his legs over the side of the bed. "Tell me."

"Tell you what?"

"Whatever it is you find so damn important to wake me."

Allgood flopped into a chair. "I have information about the Duke of Dover's trainer for you."

Titus entered the room, silently laying out Hightower's clothes. The man had been with the Duke since he attended Oxford, and by the look on his face, the majordomo was not pleased with Allgood's unannounced visit.

"Let me see, the Duke's trainer resides on his estate in Scotland and is quite mysterious."

"I wouldn't say mysterious. The man simply runs a tight ship, and doesn't wish people, particularly strangers, coming to visit and disrupt his schedule."

Hightower shook his head. "Are you going to tell me anything new? If not, I'm going to finish dressing and go down to my study where I'll write Dover a letter inquiring about putting Apollo in training with his trainer."

"Did I mention that the Duke is a cousin of my wife's?"

"No, you did not mention that. How would that help me out?"

The corners of Allgood's mouth pulled up. "I had completely forgotten they were related."

"Come on, are you going to make me drag this out of you?" Hightower asked, as Titus finished with his cravat.

"Okay, okay. Let us not get testy, old man. I may have mentioned to Hyacinth's brother last evening your bad luck with the colt, and you were looking to ship him off for training. That's when he reminded me, he and Hyacinth were cousins of the Duke, and that he would be happy to send a letter of introduction on your behalf."

"That could be huge. I must thank him."

"You can do that tomorrow evening. Peter has invited the Duke and his daughter to dinner at my home tomorrow."

"This is great news, especially since we've both heard how cautious the Duke is."

"I'm sure if he decides it, Apollo will find himself in Scotland in a matter of weeks. Problem solved."

"It certainly would be."

"Well, have you any appointments this morning, correspondence to catch up on?"

"I have no appointments, and going through my correspondence should take little time," Hightower replied, arching an eyebrow. "What exactly do you have in mind?"

"I thought we could go to White's for lunch, and then on to Tattersall's afterwards," Allgood said.

"That would be reasonable. I understand the Marquess of Leeds has brought a couple of thoroughbreds to Tattersall's. They're Irish, and the bloodlines are what I desire. I'd like to at least look."

Allgood headed to the door. "What are we waiting for? Let's go to your study so you can open your blasted correspondence. Then on to White's for lunch."

Shaking his head, Hightower followed his friend out of his bedchamber, leaving Titus to clean up.

They entered his study and while Hightower sat behind his desk to open his correspondence, Allgood found a book, and was restlessly flipping through the pages as he sat in front of the small fire. Hightower noted his friend was easily bored. The book didn't hold his attention, but then, Allgood had never been a ravenous reader. Even as far back as their days at Eton, Allgood had struggled with their reading assignments.

Hightower was the exact opposite, loving nothing better than to spend a quiet evening at home reading, either in his library or study. He continued looking over his morning correspondence. There were invitations to a few balls and a musicale, but nothing overly important.

There was only one ball out of four he wished to attend now, and the musicale wouldn't hold his interest. Most were performances given by eager mothers, wanting to see their daughters married to the highest-ranking peer they could muster. The trouble was most of the young ladies in question were poorly lacking in talent.

"Are you going to attend any of the balls?" his friend asked.

"Perhaps the Duke and Duchess of Liverpool's annual ball. I haven't decided."

Allgood smiled all knowingly. "A good one to be seen at. Everyone who's anyone will be there."

A footman entered the room with a tray containing tea, along with toast and jam. Hightower rarely ate a large meal early in the morning. The footman set the tray down and began to place the newspapers on the corner of Hightower's desk.

"Hand them to Lord Allgood. I'm sure the reading is far better suited to him than the book he is attempting to read."

Allgood set the book down and took the papers from the young man. "It's too early to be delving into such intense subject matter."

Hightower waited for the footman to leave. He rose from his desk to pour himself a cup of tea, leaving Allgood to pour his own. "I'm sure it is. Gossip can be so much more entertaining, don't you think?"

"Not everything printed in the newspapers is gossip you know."

"Agreed," Hightower replied, picking up a piece of buttered toast. He really needed to do better about his eating habits. People waking him early and changing his routine didn't help.

Hightower had always been amazed by how lackadaisical his friend could be about his business affairs. Allgood had plenty to divert his attention but seemed to need more time to play than he did. The hours and hours his friend had spent working on some major projects when his father had been alive were to be commended. It was either one of two ways with his friend. He was either on top of whatever had his attention, or he showed a huge lack of interest, acting quite bored for having been taken away from fun and games.

"Did you know Lord Keller was seen leaving one of those gaming hells?"

"Really? Which one?"

"It does not mention the actual name of the establishment, only that it's near Grosvenor square. Which means it most likely must be The Three Horsemen. It's the only place I know, er, have heard of in that vicinity."

"I'm sure. Anything else noteworthy going on?" he asked Allgood as he returned to his desk to sip his tea and finish his correspondence. If he could get his friend to quiet down, he'd get through this a lot faster.

"I know you're not interested, though if you're ever going to find a wife, you might start paying attention."

Sebastian shook his head. "We've been over this numerous times. Stop trying to marry me off."

Allgood arched a brow. "Sebastian, what you need to do is hire yourself a man to take care of the more mundane areas of your life. Give yourself a chance to live."

"I am living, Crispin. Perhaps not in the manner *you* would, but I'm content. And should I ever need assistance, Titus is quite capable of helping me out."

Allgood didn't answer, their conversation long forgotten as he turned to a new page in one of the newspapers. Hightower knew to finish up his tasks quickly.

If he let Crispin continue, it would be a late lunch they enjoyed.

The next few minutes were relegated to relative silence. If one could consider the regular sound of a newspaper's pages being turned, or the hefty sighs that filled the room on occasion. "Why don't you pour yourself a cup of tea and stop moaning like an old lady. I promise all that noise isn't going to motivate me into going any faster."

"I'll have you know I don't moan... at least not unless it involves a member of the opposite sex."

Sebastian put his hand up. "Enough! I really am not in the mood to listen about your sexual exploits."

The room remained silent until Titus entered the room. Hightower handed the majordomo the finished correspondence and set his pen aside. No words were exchanged between the two men. Titus had been in his employ long enough that he knew most everything about the Duke.

"I've done all I can do. If you've finished with your gossip sheets, we can leave for White's."

Allgood quickly folded the newspaper and rose from the chair he'd been occupying. "Thank goodness. I was afraid you were going to be at least another hour, and we might have to wait."

"I have no doubt you'd do your best to make sure we don't wait."

"Yes. I hate to wait. Especially when it involves a good meal."

"If you don't quit your ways you're going to end up like your father, Crispin," Hightower muttered.

Allgood's late father had been known to overindulge quite frequently. He had been prone to bouts of gout, and Lord knew what else. Crispin tried, and for the most part, walked a straight line at home.

Whenever Hyacinth was away, it was as though some other animal was unleashed, which led to some nocturnal activities not even Hightower could stomach.

"I know, I know. You, my friend, need to lighten up. Acting so dowdy, you will never find a wife. You'll run off all the young ladies."

"As you keep harping about. Can we please change the subject?"

"To what?"

"Are you still going to those fights?"

Allgood nodded with a smile. "Yes, though my wife has tried to convince me not to partake."

"Is it working?"

"No. I find it an excellent way to relax."

Hightower bit back a laugh. "I can assure you I could find something far more entertaining to find to relax."

"Such as? A horse ride, most likely."

"Why not? It beats getting beat up," he replied.

HE AND CRISPIN moved on to Tattersall's after a large lunch at White's, complete with whiskey and wine. Sebastian honestly did not know how his friend could hold his alcohol so well this early in the day. He only partook during the day if it were regarding business or extremely cold. Consuming alcohol during the day for pleasure was not in his makeup. It made him sleepy, and then a nap was what he preferred to do. His days of being a rakehell were over; he'd put that time in his life behind him for his sisters.

They took their time looking at what was being offered. The mares, along with one young stallion from the Marquess of Leed's farm caught his eye.

They were magnificent Irish Thoroughbreds. Adding at least one of the mares to his fledgling herd might be wise. The mare he was interested in was a deep red chestnut, with a white stocking on the back leg and a white sock on the opposite front. A large star dotted between her eyes. The stallion he currently used for breeding was getting on in age, and he was Arabian. If he were able to breed with this mare, he should have a most athletic flat racer.

The stallion was eye catching; a large black with four white stockings and a narrow blaze down the middle of his face. He had been raced once, a month ago, and came in a close second, which made Hightower curious as to why the Marquess would want to part with such a promising youngster.

Hearing a woman's voice he turned to see whom Allgood was speaking to. As he turned, his eyes locked on the young woman. The woman from the race. The one who had been screaming at the horses as they flew by. She was trying to get a better look at the stallion he was interested in, as a man he recognized to be the Duke of Dover was conversing with Crispin.

He caught Allgood's eye. He indeed wanted to be introduced, and to know who she was to the Duke. Hightower recalled hearing something about the Duke's wife dying but couldn't recall the reason.

"Hightower, may I present George Keats, Duke of Dover, and his daughter, Lady Cora," Allgood said. "Your Grace, Sebastian Steele, Duke of Hightower."

Dover nodded recognizing Sebastian. "Yes, we've worked together in Parliament a couple of times."

"It was an honor, Your Grace," Sebastian replied. "What brings you to Tattersall's this afternoon?"

"Word had it the Marquess of Leeds had a few

horses here. My daughter convinced me we should look."

"Yes, they are magnificent. Excellent blood lines," Hightower replied. He felt Lady Cora's eyes burning right through him. Obviously the lady also had a fondness for a good horse.

"You know good racing bloodlines, Your Grace?" she asked, oh, so innocently.

"I've always had an eye for fine horseflesh, my lady. Horses are a passion of mine."

She arched a brow before addressing her father. "I think we should purchase all three."

Surprisingly The, the Duke nodded and said nothing for a moment, while his daughter stepped in for a closer look. "Allgood tells me you wish to discuss placing a young stallion with my trainer."

"Yes. I believe he needs someone who isn't so close to work with him until he gets out of whatever it is he's going through."

The older man nodded understanding what Hightower was conveying. Anyone who knew racehorses would. "We'll discuss it at dinner tomorrow. My trainer is quite choosy on what horses are brought into training. We can talk and see if your stallion might be right."

It was time to leave. The Duke's attention was with his daughter, and he and Allgood had interrupted their time together. Tomorrow would be soon enough. Right now, though, he had three horses to see about purchasing.

"You're going to purchase all three?" Allgood gasped in amazement. "Why?"

"They have impeccable bloodlines and are exactly what I need. My stallion is up there in years, and I don't know how long I'll be able to make use of him," he said. He was going to mention his opinion that he thought the Duke's daughter was spoiled but refrained. If he were honest with himself, he wasn't sure how he felt. She was attractive, confident, and certainly opinionated.

"What will you do with him? "

"Put him out to pasture to live out the remainder of his life. Perhaps ride him from time to time," Sebastian replied.

"But what of Apollo? I thought you were going to use him for breeding?"

Sebastian smiled. "I intend to, but not until he's proven himself on the track."

"Ah yes. Now I recall." He turned to look back at the Duke's daughter, who was eyeing one of the Marquess's mares. "Come you better find out about purchasing them. The Duke's daughter seems to also have a keen interest with them."

"Which I find quite unusual. Very unbecoming for a highborn young woman like her, don't you think?"

"Now that you mention it, yes, it is unnerving, but I've heard the Duke indulges his daughter."

"Do you know how well she rides?" Sebastian found himself asking.

"No, but at least now you know who the mysterious lady at the rail was."

His lips curved up slightly thinking about that afternoon, and how the dark-haired beauty enthusiastically cheered her father's horse on as it won. "Yes, I do."

Allgood frowned at him. "I don't like it when you look like that."

"Like what?"

"Like you just woke up from a naughty schoolboy dream."

Sebastian lifted a brow. "That's contemptible. Give me a little more credit than that. I scarcely know the chit."

"When did that ever stop you?" Crispin bit off, attempting unsuccessfully not to laugh.

Sebastian stared harshly at his friend. "I'll pretend I didn't hear that. Now, come. Before the Duke's daughter convinces her father *she* must have them. By the way what was her name?"

"Cora. Her name's Cora."

Hightower smirked as he passed his friend to make an inquiry with a Tattersall's agent. "Cora, that's right." He would have to return to sign the remaining paperwork for the horses, but at least for now, he'd ensured the sale after putting a large deposit on the trio.

3

Hightower arrived at the townhome Allgood and his wife were renting while their home was undergoing renovations. With the countess away, Allgood had complained about the frivolous expense, boasting he could have stayed at Yorkshire House, his London residence. The countess however had other plans.

He handed his hat, gloves, and greatcoat off to the butler, and followed the gray-haired gentleman to the drawing room doors, where he was announced. Sometimes societal etiquette was ostentatious and completely unnecessary. His lips quivered, anticipating what the Duke's daughter's reaction had been when she discovered the three horses owned by the Marquess of Leeds had been sold out from under her. Most likely she had been fuming upon hearing the news.

He would have to be on his guard this evening, as Allgood had informed him the Duke's daughter despised losing at anything.

He surveyed the room quickly as he strode in deeper. Allgood and his cousin were in front of the hearth deep in conversation with the Duke. Lady Cora listened attentively.

She was exquisite, even dazzling to look at, dressed in a dark-red silk gown that showed more cleavage than Hightower thought appropriate for such a young woman. He wondered what her story was.

What sort of secrets was she hiding?

Her dark hair was swept up, while a ruby necklace graced her long, elegant neck.

Once introductions were made, he gratefully accepted a glass of whiskey from Allgood. His friend's face said it all. Lady Cora was not amused upon learning all three of those horses belonging to the Marquess of Leeds had been sold out from under her. And to none other than him.

It hadn't occurred to him until now that he might have marred his chances at placing Apollo with the Duke's trainer. Lady Cora surely wouldn't have that much influence over her father. Or did she?

Perhaps if he paid little attention to her for now, it would allow him time to judge her reaction, or lack of it. Apart from the horses at Tattersall's, he hadn't done anything to slight her. At least he couldn't think of anything he might have done.

"We were just discussing the Duke of Liverpool's up-and-coming stallion," Allgood said. "He's got great potential."

Lady Cora's lips pursed, as though she desperately wanted to say something, but was holding back. Was it because her father told her to be on her best behavior, or did she merely think her father's stable far superior? She was a hard woman to read. It wasn't that she wasn't appealing or even a gorgeous woman; there was just something about her he hadn't been able to quite put his finger on.

"Tell me about this young stallion you feel needs use of my trainer?" Dover asked. "From what Allgood has told me, he had great potential and suddenly lost interest. Perhaps he's bored. It's been known to happen."

"I've thought of that. It came about suddenly about two or three races ago. He lived to race, and then all of a sudden, he lost interest, like you said. I've tried changing riders with no luck. I'm too close and can't look at him objectively."

The Duke nodded thoughtfully. "Yes, I can see where that could happen. Allgood says he was orphaned, and you raised him yourself?"

"Yes, which is why I need to step back from his training."

"Viscount Ellsworth has an excellent trainer from what I understand. Perhaps that would be the best course for your stallion," Lady Cora said.

Sebastian's neck snapped around to look at her. Her face was a mask, and her voice was full of disdain. "I'm sorry, my lady, but you would know this—how?"

"It's an age-old problem with thoroughbreds. If they aren't stimulated, they grow bored. They're hot-blooded, just like Arabians."

"Or he could be in some discomfort?" Dover added.

"I've had him thoroughly checked by two veterinarians. Everything has been done."

"Maybe you should just accept the fact that this stallion of yours isn't as born for racing as you think, Your Grace," Lady Cora murmured.

Sebastian bristled at her malicious remark, but remained stoic, ignoring her, not wishing to harm his fledgling relationship with her father. He held the key to putting in a good word or even a recommendation to his trainer.

Whatever reason she had for that acid tongue, he would find out. It would take a strong man to deal with her. His best remedy would be to not engage her in conversation. Whatever her reason, she was trying extremely hard not to like him.

He knew Allgood and Viscount Cecil were watching him closely, wondering if the old Hightower would emerge and say something equally scathing to her, or if he would simply choose to ignore her.

Fortunately, before he could reply, the butler announced dinner was ready, leaving him the opening he'd been hoping for. He followed everyone. Allgood wasn't one for formalities, especially with his wife out of town.

Lady Cora had been placed directly across from him, seated next to the Viscount. He exhaled a sigh of relief. The Duke was seated to his left, making it perfect for the two to get to know each other better. The Duke had many interests besides his horses, Hightower soon learned. He was intrigued to learn Dover had a keen interest in horticulture. He also boasted a renowned collection of artwork by Dutch masters he'd been collecting over the years, along with a small collection of Ming vases. Hightower was enthralled by the paintings the Duke possessed. While he enjoyed fine artwork, he'd had little time to procure pieces for his country estate. The collection of Ming vases equally fascinated him. He had acquired three pieces over the past few years, which were displayed in a locked glass case in the library.

Dover waited for the footman to place the soup before him. Sebastian slyly cut a look at Lady Cora, to find her engaged in conversation with Allgood. Better him. He was still reeling from her remark. He pitied any man who might be attracted to her.

"Hightower here has a few pieces of Ming, don't you?" Allgood inquired.

"Yes. Unfortunately, with Ming there is a huge counterfeit market, and one has to either have an expert to assist with the purchase or know how to spot a fake on their own, which involves knowing where to look."

"Are you sure they're the genuine article?" Lady Cora asked.

"Yes," he replied curtly, directing his attention to the soup before him.

Dover looked up from his bowl. "If I remember correctly, your grandmother had the most magnificent rose garden at Hightower Hall."

Sebastian glanced at Dover. "Yes. In fact, a few of her roses still produce some of the best blooms."

"I take it you've kept the gardens up?"

"Yes, my mother also had a keen fondness for roses. I guess I picked up my interest from them."

"I remember being in awe when I saw them many years ago. My late wife and I had been invited to one of your parents' famous summer parties."

"My sisters and I were on our best behavior, or else we found ourselves looking out at the festivities from the nursery windows," he replied. "We were allowed to mingle among the guests for about an hour each afternoon."

"Why don't you carry on the tradition, Hightower?" Allgood teased.

"Perhaps once I marry, or if one of my sisters marries first, I'll resume the tradition."

"You have three sisters?" Lady Cora inquired. Hightower cringed at what might come out of her mouth. It seemed she had nothing nice to say about anyone.

"Yes. Lady Beatrice is two years older than I, and Ladies Theodora and Matilda follow me as the two youngest."

"So you have no heir." She smirked.

"No, not at present, as I've never married."

Hightower thought the evening would never progress, that dinner would never end. Though the Duke and he seemed to be hitting it off, he had no idea where he stood in getting Apollo a spot with the Duke's elusive trainer.

She appeared to be an intelligent young woman. One who wasn't afraid to voice her own opinions, which he did find refreshing. To a point. Lady Cora could be sharp-tongued, in spite of the fact she was quite beautiful and self-assured. He found himself wanting to know more about her, although a voice inside his head told him to beware of her.

Horses had not been talked about since Lady Cora's scathing comment. Hightower hoped while the gentlemen took brandy and cigars, the subject might be broached once again.

He listened as she spoke with Allgood and Cecil about hot air balloons being demonstrated each afternoon in Hyde Park. He'd seen them twice as his sisters Theodora and Matilda pestered him to no end until he gave in and took them. They had been amazing, and the girl's mesmerized by them.

He studied her from hooded eyes, only to find she was observing him in much the same manner. She immediately looked away when she caught him looking at her. Hightower had to admit she did intrigue, though he would never let her know. He felt the pull of attraction this evening harder to dismiss.

She wasn't at all the sort of woman he might choose, and in spite of her acid tongue, he found himself quite drawn to her, wondering what sort of woman she really was under the hard veneer she surrounded herself with.

He smiled at her for a second, only to let her know she'd be caught. Obviously, she wasn't used to anyone challenging her, and though he did so without words, Hightower did challenge her and whatever her motive was.

Though Allgood asked him to wait until after the Duke and his daughter left, he did so grudgingly. He didn't need to sit around with the two while they tried to figure out what he really thought of Dover's daughter.

"Good evening, Your Grace," Lady Cora said as they were preparing to leave. "It was nice to meet you again. I wish you luck with your stallion. I'm sure there's someone out there willing to take him on. I'm afraid he wouldn't be worth our trainer's time. You understand, I'm sure." Her eyes sparkled with mischief.

What her father needed to do was turn her over his knee and give her a good thrashing. Maybe then she'd learn to curve her tongue and not embarrass her father.

"Nice to meet you, Lady Cora. I'm sure we'll meet again. Soon," he replied, his lips curved up slightly as the words left his mouth. Let her think she had the upper hand.

He lingered in the drawing room, pouring himself another brandy waiting for Allgood and the others to return. He sat down in a dark-blue damask chair and crossed his legs.

"I dare say, Lady Cora was not amused that you

purchased all three of those horses from under her father," the Viscount said as he and Allgood returned.

"No, I'm sure she wasn't, and I have to finalize the sale in the morning. I really don't understand why she insists on inserting herself in matters best left to men," Hightower murmured.

"She is spoiled and headstrong," Allgood replied.

"She needs a good thrashing," Hightower grunted as he took as sip of his brandy.

"The introduction has been made; the Duke will present the idea to his trainer. It's just a matter of waiting," the Viscount said. "As for Lady Cora and her say in the matter, she's all talk."

"So I gather, though her smart mouth does grow tiresome," Hightower added.

"She's a pretty little thing," Allgood said. He winked at Sebastian, who simply shook his head and emptied his glass.

"Pretty doesn't help with a mouth like that. It is no wonder she isn't married. What man would want to listen to that? She holds nothing back."

The viscount offered him another brandy. "I don't remember her being quite so harsh. Opinionated, yes, but never like this. It might be something that's manifested itself since the death of her mother."

"That very well could be," Hightower mused.

"When do you plan to return to your estate?" Allgood asked.

"I was planning on leaving in the morning, after I finish my business at Tattersall's. Apollo needs to be in the country while I figure out what to do with him."

"Pity. You'll miss out on all the balls and soirees." Allgood grinned.

Sebastian shook his head. "Don't worry. I'll be back

within a fortnight. I accepted an invitation to the Duke and Duchess of Liverpool's annual ball."

"Yes, Hyacinth plans to return if possible. If she hasn't, I'll go on my own. It's one of the most sought-after invitations."

"They do invite a crush," Cecil added.

"That they do, which is one reason I go. Everyone is there, so I tell myself I don't need to attend any others," Sebastian said.

"I've always found Liverpool's timing odd. Most people have left town, yet everyone comes rushing back just to be seen at his ball," Allgood said.

"Powerful and well-liked man," Hightower replied.

"Yes, that's what it must be," Allgood agreed. "Are you planning to look for an alternative trainer, just in case Dover's doesn't have time?"

"I know of no one else I want to work with him. If Dover's trainer doesn't have time, I'll let Apollo have some time off, a month or two, then I'll restart working him myself."

"You know him better than anyone. That might be all it takes. A good rest in one of your meadows."

"For now, I'll play the waiting game. We'll return to the country tomorrow and see if that doesn't change his disposition."

"Horses are such fickle creatures," Allgood sighed.

"Says the man who knows nothing about them."

Allgood shook his head before putting it back and laughing. "What's there to know. A groom brings me my gelding, I mount him, ride him, and return him to the mews. That's all I need to know. I even have my stablemaster pick out my carriage and riding horses."

"That's because you know no better," Hightower snorted.

"No, I simply don't have the interest you do."

"Yes, your interests lie elsewhere," Sebastian replied with a smile.

Cecil sat back on the settee. "Dover didn't seem too upset by the fact you'd purchased all three of those horses."

"Of course, he wasn't. It was his daughter who wanted them, not he," Sebastian quipped.

"When will they go to your estate?" Allgood inquired.

"In two days. I must finalize the sale in the morning. Seems the Marquess left word he was to be consulted on where the animals went. I sent word to let them know to expect them."

"I'm surprised Lady Cora didn't try and talk you into selling one of them to her father," Cecil said.

"I think she knew better than to test my patience further," Hightower replied.

"Perhaps," Allgood added. "Or she knew tonight wasn't the right time."

Sebastian arched a brow. "She didn't let anything else stop her this evening. If she really wanted one, she'd have her father approach me. The lady may be pretty, but she's nobody's fool."

4

Hightower arrived at Tattersall's the next morning to take care of the final paperwork on the three horses he'd purchased.

He was led into a private office, bank draft in hand for the remaining balance, not uncommon, as this was a rather large transaction. He was standing in front of a large oak desk admiring the many drawings hanging on the walls, when a gentleman he recognized as Horatio Bottoms, one of the managers of Tattersall's, entered the office.

"Good morning, Your Grace," Bottoms said, bowing slightly. He was an older, muscular man, who'd worked his way through the ranks at this fine establishment to get to where he was. He was well known as an excellent trainer of carriage horses, especially teams of four.

"Good morning. I trust everything is in order?"

Bottoms adverted his eyes looking at the paperwork on his desk. He'd known Bottoms long enough to know something was not right. He'd hired the man on several occasions for one thing or another, regarding carriage horses or the vehicles they pulled, and Bottoms had always been a self-assured, confident man. The man in front of him was nervous.

"Why don't we sit down, Your Grace," he said. "I'm afraid there's a slight problem regarding the horses you wish to purchase."

Hightower sat up ramrod straight and stared at the man. "What sort of problem?"

Diverting his eyes from Hightower, the man continued. "It seems the Marquess has chosen to sell his horses to someone else. I only just found out about it this morning when I arrived. I sent someone to your house to stop you from making the trip, but you had already left."

Sucking in a deep breath, Hightower nodded at the unexpected news. This was not the man's fault. It was out of his hands, and Hightower couldn't blame him. The Marquess was an odd man anyway when it came to his horses.

Apollo was his primary focus. Taking him home and letting him enjoy his freedom until he heard back from Dover, or he found someone else. The stallion and two mares would have been a nice addition to his stable, but he would continue looking.

"Do you know whom he sold them to? I only ask because I like to know who my competition is."

"I do not, Your Grace. It seems the Marquess is taking control of the entire transaction. All I know is to release them when the new owners arrive to the loading area with their bill of sale. That's all the marquess told us."

"I see," Hightower replied. "Do not worry over it. It was a spur of the moment decision. I'm sure I'll find something to replace them."

"Please feel free to look, Your Grace. There are some excellent mares and stallions to choose from, and we're expecting some Irish Thoroughbreds later in the week."

"Maybe I shall. I won't take up any more of your time, Bottoms. I know you're a busy man."

"Thank you, Your Grace, and again I'm sorry this happened and hope it doesn't reflect badly on Tattersall's."

Hightower shook his head and stood. "Not at all."

"Your Grace, I almost forgot...your deposit." He handed a bank draft to Sebastian.

"Thank you, Bottoms."

He left the office, resigned to what had just happened. He had been outmaneuvered, and that alone didn't sit well with him.

Something near the rear door caught his eye. There was always a lot of activity in this area, and he immediately recognized two of the Marquess's horses.

His curiosity piqued, he drew closer. Would the new owners themselves come to pick them up, or send a groom? He would try to inquire with a couple of the young lads and see where the Marquess's horses were headed. Not that it was any of his concern, but he was curious to know who'd outbid him or convinced the Marquess into selling the lot to them.

As he discreetly attempted to look outside, his eyes locked with Lady Cora Keats, the daughter of the Duke of Dover, who looked smug and triumphant over her father's new purchase.

He simply tipped his hat and walked off, knowing if he said a word, he might live to regret it. He was still interested in seeing if the Duke's trainer would accept Apollo, so bickering with his daughter over horses she had to have was not in his best interest.

He knew when to cut his losses, and this was one

of them. All he knew was that Lady Cora Keats was a pain in his arse.

He found his horse and left for an appointment with his solicitor about a business opportunity he was interested in investing in. Electricity. There was an American inventor who was at the forefront of this, and Hightower wanted in. If he could invest in this man's companies and vision, he would become wealthier than could be imagined. The world was moving ahead, and he knew he could no longer rely on his estates or other safe investments as his father and grandfather had. Certainly he would continue to profit from them, but it was time to join the industrial revolution.

This morning, he sat in the office of Anthony Banks, the younger of the brothers. He sat in front of the large oak desk as the man had gone to find the paperwork pertinent to the inventor and his companies. He knew the financing was secure.

By the time their meeting concluded, Hightower had everything he needed in hand. His two partners were on the Continent on another matter and had left it to him to make whatever decisions were needed. He would write and tell them what transpired today. They were moving ahead with their plans.

His majordomo would prepare his things, and he would leave first thing in the morning. By the time he arrived at Hightower Hall, there would plenty of time for him to catch up on estate matters. The sooner he put distance between him and Lady Cora, the better, and he hoped he never ran into the chit again. She was an obnoxious, spoiled, mettlesome thing who needed a good dressing-down and put in her place by her father.

He pitied the man who ended up her husband.

The man would have to have the patience of an oak to put up with her. Hopefully, once word arrived to Dover's trainer, and the man accepted taking Apollo into training, he wouldn't run into Lady Cora. Surely she had too many other people to torment.

As he dismounted in front of his London home, it occurred to him he was hungry. In his anger about being outdone by Lady Cora's father, Sebastian had totally forgotten to stop for lunch. He would soon remedy the matter.

Even better, he knew of no engagements he had tonight. He would enjoy nothing better than to spend a quiet evening at home with a novel and his best brandy. Not even Allgood could persuade him to leave the comforts of his home.

His trip to Hightower Hall was not as planned. Bad weather put a halt to his riding back. Instead, he sat in his carriage, the curtains drawn to keep out the dampness. The novel he'd begun the night before proved to be more entertaining than he first thought it would be, and he brought it along to pass the time.

He could tell once they were on the outskirts of London. The traffic thinned out and the cobblestones became packed dirt roads. Lifting one curtain he peered outside. The rain still came down at a good pace. Hopefully, they'd make his estate before the roads started to get really muddy. Of all the estates he possessed, Hightower Hall was by far his favorite. It was the ducal family home, which might explain why he felt the way he did. It had been where he and his sisters had been raised.

The house would be quiet, his sisters having left to

spend a good portion of the summer in Bath. Their late mother's sister, Viscountess Makemark, had invited them sometime earlier, and he agreed it would do them good to see something other than Hightower Hall. Theodora and Matilda were of age to have their first season. He'd put theirs off, because in his opinion, they weren't mature enough to be put on the marriage mart. Beatrice had enjoyed two seasons but had sat out of any more. She seemed content bossing her sisters about, as she took her part as the oldest very seriously. Hightower smiled at the thought of Beatrice trying to order *him* about, forgetting that even though he was younger than she, he was a duke. Once she came to rights with that, the two got along famously, though unfortunately his sister had unsuccessfully tried to play matchmaker and had to be reminded that wasn't her job.

He sat back against the squabs in the corner of the carriage and picked up the novel he'd earlier placed on the seat. About a chapter into it, he felt his eyes growing heavy. Long carriage rides did that to him, which was part of the reason he rode. He hated falling asleep in the middle of the day, but on many an occasion, it saved him from conversations he didn't wish to take part in. Today, however, he cursed the affliction. He wished to get further into his book. It was rare that he had this much time to indulge himself in something as simple as reading for pleasure.

His body, however, had other plans, and soon the book fell to the floor, as Hightower fell sound asleep. He dreamt of Lady Cora. This time she was laughing at him. She made a fool of him in taking the Marquess's horses from under him. The less he saw of that obnoxious woman, the better. It mattered not to him she was a duke's daughter. She was not the sort of woman he wished to be associated with, and hopefully the incident at Tattersall's was the last time he'd have to deal with her. Surely, should Dover's trainer accept Apollo, he wouldn't have to see her. The farm and training facility was in Scotland, and he couldn't imagine the chit wanting anything to do with being sent to some far remote estate.

Without warning, the carriage went through a pothole in the road and came to a groaning halt, listing as it came to a stop. In the pouring-down rain. He donned his hat and opened the door. The driver and two footmen stood on the opposite side, two of them bent down inspecting the carnage.

A wheel had broken, and any attempt to move it from the pothole would result in the carriage collapsing.

He surveyed the wheel himself. It would require someone going to the nearest village and finding a wheelwright. Sebastian looked around trying to get his bearings. There was nothing but farmland for miles. Endless fields and grassy meadows surrounded him. It was midafternoon, and he knew of two villages not far off.

"Send a man to one of the villages. If he can't find a wheelwright, have him move on to the next," he said to the driver. "There is a spare horse he can ride isn't there?"

"Yes, Your Grace. I'll send Charles immediately."

"Very well. I'm going to ride on, since Hightower Hall isn't too far. I'll send another carriage once I arrive with more men to help."

"Very well, Your Grace."

One of the footmen brought his mount to him. He pulled the collar of his great coat up, put on his black leather gloves and made sure his hat was securely in place. Hightower swung his leg over the beast and began to ride. Despite the cold, biting rain he pushed on. Then he urged his mount into a gallop. With any luck he would arrive soon.

Blast! This was exactly why he shouldn't have sent the second carriage with his man and trunks on before him, but he knew Titus was impatient and wanted to have him settled by the time he returned home. Accidents happened, but never to him. He couldn't recall the last time he'd had a wheel break. His staff kept his carriages and horses in meticulous shape; he liked to think they were some of the more meticulous ones in all of London.

Blast it all. Now he had this bother to deal with, riding in the pouring rain. For once he was thankful no one would be at home when he arrived soaked to the skin. It would be bad enough that Titus would fuss over him, his sisters would be relentless, wanting to play nurse to him if they were at home. They didn't understand he was a grown man of twenty-seven, and a duke. He was perfectly capable of taking care of himself.

The rain pelted down, hitting his face as the winds picked up, and with it the rain. For a few minutes he thought about stopping and waiting under a tree until the rain subsided. He decided against it.

He pushed the animal on. The roads were beginning to turn to mud from the force and amount of rain. Soon he recognized the large rolling fields that ran down to the road. The rock fence walls appeared, and the oak-lined drive welcomed him. He guided his mount on to the long drive and slowed him down, despite the fact the rain had yet to stop or even slow down. He'd pushed him hard enough and walking or even a slow trot up to the house was the least he could do. He wasn't going to get any drier or warmer, but the horse had done what he'd asked without hesitation.

The front door opened as they came up to the front of the house. Davis, Hightower Hall's butler, must have been watching from one of the windows because the man flung open the door and quickly had a stable boy scurrying down the stairs to take care of his horse.

He passed the horse to the young boy, telling him to give his mount a good rub down and an extra ration of oats.

Hightower sprinted up the stairs and through the open door, handing Davis his hat. He removed his gloves and placed them on the table, then let the butler assist him out of his rain-soaked greatcoat.

Out of the corner of his eye he noticed Titus shaking his head in disapproval.

"Damn carriage wheel broke in a pothole."

"Do I need to send help, Your Grace?"

He nodded. "Have some men take a spare carriage. It might take a wheelwright a while to get to them and there's no reason for them to sit around in the rain waiting."

"Very well, Your Grace."

Titus edged closer. "Should I draw a bath for you, Your Grace?"

"Yes. I need to get out of these wet clothes before I do anything else," he replied. Turning to the butler, he continued. "I'm afraid I haven't eaten since this morning. See that a tray of cheese and bread and fruit are sent to my sitting room. Hot tea as well."

He didn't hear what the butler said as he continued across the hall to the grand staircase. Titus had long disappeared. The man was good at doing that. Hightower took the stairs two at a time again. For once he was glad to be home and couldn't wait until he checked in on Apollo to see how the youngster was doing.

~

LADY CORA STOOD hands on her hips as she watched her newest acquisitions being led into their respective stalls inside the large stables. The two mares and stallion seemed to be grateful for the room of their stalls after having endured the long journey from London to Lanarkshire, Scotland.

She smiled, remembering the Duke of Hightower's face when their eyes locked at the doorway of Tattersall's, and he realized she and her father had convinced the Marquess to sell the lot to them, rather than him. He had looked furious, his eyes dark as storm clouds.

He'd been mistaken if he thought he could try and purchase the horses from under her. It hadn't taken much for her father to convince the Marquess to reconsider. She was known for being a spoiled and overindulged young lady, and it had proven to work in her favor this time. She wanted something, and she got it. the Duke of Hightower be damned!

Fortunately for her, her father had seen the talent she possessed with training horses, racers in particular. The horses she'd trained were consistent winners, and future stud fees would put her father's line on the map.

The Duke of Dover, knowing women were limited, had agreed to split all fees and sales equally with her. Her portion was deposited into her bank account.

Knowing it was unheard of that a horse trainer was a woman, especially a duke's daughter, made things more interesting. To get over some men's hesitation about a woman trainer, they kept the farm closed to all outsiders. Horses that were accepted were done so carefully. The horses shipped directly to Scotland, where they underwent rigorous training without interference from their owners. When finished, her stable master would either ship the animal back to its owner, or if the owner insisted on seeing the progress on the farm, Dougan MacTavish would meet with the owners. The elusive trainer "G.S." would always be away at a race or some other matter that wouldn't raise suspicions.

Which brought her back to the Duke of Hightower, and his wish to send his stallion to the farm for evaluation and possible training. The stallion was good; she'd seen him race several times, but he appeared to have lost interest the past few races.

While she had said nothing, she suspected the colt was simply bored and needed a month or so off. For now, she would keep the Duke dangling, as he'd already written G.S. requesting to send the beast.

Her father told her she was playing with fire, but she dismissed it after seeing the look of fury on the Duke's face. He was going to make a worthy opponent.

As she only took on two horses at a time so that she didn't ignore her own stallion's needs, she would wait until one left in a couple of weeks. Then she would decide for certain whether to take on Hightower's horse. It wasn't like she didn't have horses to choose from. For now, she'd send him a letter, telling him she didn't have room, but would reply with her answer as soon as she sent one of her two charges home. That ought to pacify Hightower.

She walked over to one of the mare's stalls and opened it slowly. The stall had been deeply bedded and hay had been thrown in one corner. She was a beautiful, well-boned mare, and would serve her well when she went to breed St. Elmo's Fire.

Quietly she closed the door, walked over to the next stall, and went through the procedure again. Again, the mare was settling in—eating, though a bit skittish. That would dissipate in a day or two, once she became familiar with her new surroundings.

Walking over to the stallion, whose stall was at the end on the opposite side, she peered inside. He was pacing the large stall, picking up a mouthful of hay, then continuing his pacing. Tomorrow, after he had time to settle in from the long journey, she would have him put out in the paddock that was accessible through the second door in his stall. Normally the tops of the doors were left open but since he was new, she thought it best if he spent a quiet night. No need to get him stirred up with more new and unfamiliar sights. It was best to introduce him slowly.

Finley, one of their large Scottish deerhounds, came bounding through the door. He took one look and ran to her. She gave him lots of pats and hugs, wondering what sort of mischief Zeus might be into. The stallion snorted from behind the bars of his stall, unsure what to make of the pair.

Knowing the dog's need to chase a stick or run to tire him out, she turned and walked outside. She would walk over to her charge's paddock and see how he was progressing. In the early morning she would take him on a gallop around the track and see how much further MacTavish had gotten with him.

Though she would like nothing more than to be left to her horses and farm, unfortunately, as her father's hostess, it was virtually impossible, especially at certain times of the year. She detested the teas, luncheons, soirees, and balls he would have her attend or host for him, but she gladly did so for him. She was also aware her father was on the lookout for a suitable match for her. There was no man alive she would ever consider marrying.

She made sure she found something wrong with all the suitors presented to her. Fortunately, her father saw her objections, and the matter went no further. How much longer she could keep this up, she didn't know. She was constantly reminded she was getting older, and needed to think of her duty, but what man could accept what she had here? She had more to lose, her business, her money, and the freedom to make her own choices. She certainly wasn't going to give it up to marry some dowdy, stuffy man. Until she found him, she would continue on, doing what she loved.

Her brother Augustus faced a similar fate. As his father's heir, he needed to marry and start a family of his own, but Augustus had other plans. One day he up and left, leaving the whiskey distillery and estate, to wander the Continent with a couple of his friends. Men could do things like that. She knew though her father was disappointed in Augustus, he'd never say it out loud. Instead, he picked up the pieces and allowed his son his time.

5

"It seems the Duke of Hightower is most anxious to send his stallion here for training," her father, said, placing the letter next to her plate as he sat down across from her. A footman brought him a plate piled high with his favorites.

Cora pushed the letter aside without reading it. "He's becoming most annoying."

"We'll write him, assure him as soon as you're free of the one of your charges, you'll take on his horse."

"Fine," she replied. "It needs to be made very clear he is to send the stallion, nothing else, and that we'll inform him of the horse's progress."

The Duke smiled. "We do that with all the clients."

"Yes, but Hightower seems a little more inquisitive than most. Especially after the incident at Tattersall's."

"Why? Did something else happen?"

She shook her head of mahogany curls. "No—like I said, he's more curious than most. Most of our clients have much more to do than worry about every detail of their horses. Hightower seems a little too attached."

"We'll respond as I've outlined," her father replied. He picked up a forkful of eggs.

"Very well. I agree."

"Don't forget, we leave for the Duke and Duchess of Liverpool's ball next week."

"Papa, I know you wish to make a match for me, but I cannot continue to be absent from my work."

"In case you've forgotten, Daughter, attendance at the Liverpool ball was part of our agreement for those horses. We won't be gone long, and it'll do you good to socialize with other young men and women."

Though she loved her father with all her heart, the man could test her patience. Certainly, the horses she had under her were far enough along that her stablemaster could pick up the slack caused by her absence, but the horses also needed her expertise, and the stablemaster could not give them that.

"We'll go, but remember, when we return, you will allow me the next six weeks to devote to my training. No balls, no soirees, no teas, nothing," she finally said.

"As you wish. If you need a new gown, make arrangements with someone in Edinburgh."

She shook her head and smiled in her father's direction. "That won't be necessary, Papa. I'll wear one of the dresses I had made in Paris last winter." The gown was still fashionable by London standards. London always lagged behind Paris when it came to fashion.

"As you wish." He picked up one of his many newspapers.

Cora excused herself, but her father never acknowledged her departure. He had never been one for small talk. He would make his point or answer questions, then he withdrew into things that needed tending or made him happy.

The opportunity allowed her to make her way out to the stables. She'd already run the one stallion over the track this morning. He was making decent progress, but now they were going to mimic an actual race by adding one or two horses to move up along-side him. The stallion seemed to have a fear of that, and he would shy or slow way down, which of course put him in dead last. Their previous attempts had shown little improvement, but today she'd added blinkers, similar to what carriage horses wore. The result had been nothing short of remarkable.

She would ride the gelding, though he wasn't as enthused about racing. He went through the move-ments, but that was all. She doubted he would ever amount to much, and being a gelding, his owner would have no way of recouping the money he'd spent training him and entry fees. If she couldn't turn him around, his owner would eventually sell him.

Her mind wandered back to Hightower, making her uncomfortable. His horse was good, but she knew the Duke was already aware of that fact. He would be an interesting horse to train. A challenge, and she en-joyed a good challenge. To ride a horse of Apollo's cal-iber, feel his strength between her legs, excited her. There was nothing more exhilarating.

Hightower had changed riders, thinking that was the problem. She needed to find out who'd been riding the stallion all this time, and whom he switched to. It might be nothing, but there was always a reason why horses changed. She could make inquiries without having to ask Hightower himself. That would give her something to go on.

The stallion had been entered alongside her own on more than one occasion. She had all the paper-work. Entries, owners, jockeys, everything she would need. It could be something as easy as that. On the other hand, some horses didn't respond well to riders being changed. Hightower had indicated such. Maybe he hadn't found the right man for the job.

For now, her concern was in her barn. Once she finished with her client's horses, she could work with St. Elmo's Fire, a magnificent colt she'd picked up about a year ago. Her father had seen him race his first, how he was being held back, and knew his daughter needed him. With her expertise, she turned him into a winner. He was that good, that magnificent.

She walked the path leading to the stables. It was out of sight of the main house. Her father had built it a few years back when he realized her talent. The new building was solely for her racers, clients, and breeding stock. Everything had a place and ran like clockwork. She was meticulous that way, which might explain why she didn't care for Hightower's pushiness. He would soon see if he wanted to have his horse trained by the best, he would have to adhere to her strict rules.

It had been late before Hightower retired to his bedchamber the night before. After a long, hot bath to warm him from the bone-chilling cold the rain had brought, he found himself in a flurry of activity.

One of the first things he had done was walk back outside, much to the horror of his staff, to check on Apollo. The colt seemed to be oblivious to all the fuss, having been brought back inside. He recognized Hightower immediately and began to nicker softly, searching Sebastian's pockets for sugar cubes or slices of apple when he opened the stall door to pet the magnificent stallion.

When he'd come downstairs this morning for breakfast, the first item of business was to quickly go through the post sitting on his desk. To his disappointment no response to his letter to his request to place his colt into training had arrived.

He took his tea in his study as he slowly went through each letter. Invitations were set to one side for response, then he opened the remaining. Most were reports from some of his business ventures, and one was an inquiry from the Earl of Durham, asking if he had Apollo at stud. He thought Apollo's bloodline would work well with his mares.

Hightower took the time to respond, explaining that the colt was not quite ready to be added to his breeding program. He added a few lines about his other stallion, telling him that if the Earl were interested, he would be happy to meet with him to go over bloodlines. If not, he would keep the Earl's name on file and contact him when Apollo was ready to be sent to stud.

He reread the letter, smiling to himself. Someone had seen the youngster race and liked what they saw. The letter from the Earl only reinforced his belief in the colt.

He then turned his attention to the invitations. There was nothing that struck his interest, and he began to write his regrets.

A knock on the door forced him to look up from the desk as his stablemaster walked in. The man had grown up at Hightower Hall, his father having served Hightower's father as stablemaster. The man had grown up around the horses and had a natural touch with the animals that some simply didn't possess.

"Your Grace, I hate to disturb you, but I thought you would like to know the outcome with the carriage."

Hightower lifted a brow in interest. "Was the wheelwright able to change out the wheel?"

"Yes, your Grace. Unfortunately, the spring was damaged in all the effort to right it. I sent the carriage on to the village with the wheelwright, and had the horses returned early this morning."

"I'm sure it couldn't be avoided. The pothole was quite deep. Just make sure my other carriage is polished and cleaned. I'm sure it'll take the wheelwright several days."

The man nodded. "He did say he'd make the carriage a priority, Your Grace."

"Very well. Thank you for the update on the matter." He began to pick up his pen when it occurred to him the man was still standing in front of his desk. "Is there something else?"

"Yes, Your Grace. I wanted to clarify how the colt is to be handled. You said you wished him to have a holiday of sorts. Will you be wanting to take him out for a ride? I only ask because he can be quite a handful if he doesn't wish to be caught."

"No, I won't be riding him. Just have him let out in the morning and brought in and stalled at night. Have whoever goes after him in the evenings take a bucket of oats. That should make their job easier," he replied. "I want his mind clear when I send him off for training."

"As you wish, Your Grace. I'll instruct the lads."

"Anything else?"

"Will you be wanting to ride this afternoon?"

Hightower sat back in his chair and pondered the suggestion. He normally did ride, but earlier in the day. There were several animals he needed to ride, and since his sisters were not in residence, he would do it himself. They needed to be exercised.

"Yes, saddle Lady Beatrice's gelding for me. Have him ready in a couple of hours." He needed to take care of business before he rode. If he didn't, he found it harder to come back and resume whatever needed his attention.

"Very well, Your Grace. I'll leave you to your work," he replied.

Hightower made no sign to acknowledge the man as he quit the room. He picked up his pen and began to respond with his regrets to another soiree. A house party being held over a fortnight. He'd tried it a couple of times but found being in one location for that long as tedious at best. There was only so much charades and hunting one could endure, and most were merely ways of making matches between the single guests. Unfortunately, Hightower constantly found himself being subjected to his hostess's matchmaking, making him dislike these affairs even more.

6

Arriving in London two days prior, Hightower had told no one of his arrival except his long-time friend James Livingston, Marquess of Devon. He and Devon went back to his days at Eton, and the two of them were to become partners, investing in an American businessman and his inventions in electricity. Their mutual friend, Ronald Blair, also an American, was their third partner. He'd met the inventor and seen many of his marvels firsthand.

Devon would arrive for dinner this evening. They'd discuss their mutual investment, enjoy some brandy, and the Marquess would depart. Hightower would then be free to spend the remainder of his evening reading.

Tomorrow he would ride in Hyde Park before the Liverpool ball. After the ball, he would come straight home and go to bed. He had no time for meeting up afterwards with whatever friends showed up that evening. He wasn't here for that and planned his return to the country two days after the ball.

He requested a tray since he hadn't eaten since breakfast and spent a couple of hours reading before he dressed for dinner.

For a moment he did wonder what eligible young ladies would be attending the Liverpool ball. They would all be turned out in their finest, their doting mothers knowing the creme of the aristocracy would be in attendance. But Hightower had no desire for a debutante. He wished for someone with real world experience. Someone he could talk with on matters other than the weather or what book they had recently read.

He avoided being paired up with sisters of his friends, or anyone closely related to them. He was a duke, and he needed a duchess. A woman who stood out in a crowd, who held herself as regally as if she were a queen herself.

His friend Allgood had mentioned on more than one occasion that he would find her quite by accident. That would more than likely be the way it would occur. He'd have to be satisfied with waiting until she was presented to him.

He would know her the first time he laid eyes on her. She would have an air about her which would set her apart from the other young ladies. Hightower kept telling himself that it would be worth it. All he needed to do is be patient.

Glancing outside, he quickly decided a ride in the park would be a far more pleasant way to spend an hour or so. It was early enough that with any luck, he wouldn't run into anyone he knew. He summoned the butler to have his horse readied. Some fresh air and good weather were just what he needed.

Hyde Park wasn't far from his home, but he didn't use it nearly enough. Mainly because of the throngs of people, and though there were places he could gallop, the park still wasn't conducive to those who were there for anything other than socializing and being seen.

Walking along, deciding whether to gallop the youngster he was riding, he saw a familiar face atop a piebald horse. Lady Cora, out riding with a groom in tow.

What was she doing back in London?

He thought he'd seen the end of her, at least for now. Didn't she spend her summers at her father's estate in Scotland? What brought her back to London?

Urging the gelding on he quickly caught up with her. The look on her face when she turned and saw him was priceless.

"Your Grace," she sputtered. "I was unaware they allowed just anyone to ride these paths."

He bowed his head in recognition. "Nor I. I thought one had to be a fairly experienced rider or have someone more qualified than a groom to escort them."

"I see you came without your escort, Your Grace."

He nodded, knowing she referred to Allgood. "I did indeed, Lady Cora," he replied. "What brings you back to London so quickly? You're a long way from Scotland."

"I could ask the same of you," she said tartly, "and to answer your question, it is none of your business why I'm in London."

"I'm here on business."

"Of course you are. A typical response from a man."

His lips twitched. "Would you rather hear I'm here to visit some of the clubs I belong to?"

"The truth is always better than a lie, Your Grace."

Hightower shrugged a massive shoulder. "The truth is I'm here on business, and when I'm in London

I do frequent White's. Which, by the way, is the only club I belong."

Cora rolled her eyes. "That's what I thought, but if you did belong to any of those seedier clubs, you wouldn't tell me, would you?"

"A lady doesn't need to know such things," he replied.

"Bollocks! Women aren't some fragile pieces of porcelain. We can stand on our own two feet."

"I never said you were fragile." Lady Cora had no intention of backing down from her beliefs. Not that he'd want her to.

"I need to be on my way. I look forward to our next meeting, Good day, Lady Cora."

"Of course," she replied, pressing her heels into the piebald's side. "Good day to you, Your Grace."

She walked on, stopping at the top of a rise. She turned to find Hightower following some distance behind her. London wasn't even safe from him. Yet here he was. He seemed to love antagonizing her. He would quickly find out how little she cared about him. If she were to take his horse in for training, he wouldn't be allowed at the farm. That would rub him the wrong way. Maybe this time he would get the hint to stay a safe distance from her. He wasn't as all-important as he thought himself to be.

Looking down the path one final time she noted Hightower had disappeared. Probably off to flirt with all the ladies who were beginning to come out for their afternoon walks. Some things never changed. Young ladies came out to be seen, others were there on the arm of a hopeful intended. It was all one huge, obnoxious game. One she despised.

No one caught her fancy. Not even remotely. She knew eventually she would have to marry; it was what was expected, but if she had to, she prayed she could find a quiet, timid man. One she could overwhelm, one who would give into her whims, and most importantly, a man who would allow her to continue her training. She would become a spinster rather than marry a man who would try to make her bend to his rules. She was nobody's property, with her own money from training, and could support herself quite comfortably if she chose to leave her father's home.

Her mind wandered back to Hightower once more, which angered her. She told herself it was because he was the only unmarried man she'd had any sort of meaningful conversation with, and that appealed to her. Most men who showed any inclination of interest in her had their own motives.

The thought of the ball her father had dragged her all the way back to London to attend made her shiver. Attending was one of the few tradeoffs she made with her father, and it was worth it in the end. Even if she detested society's events, she would make it through one evening.

So here she was in London once again, forced to ride sidesaddle amongst the *ton*. If she did ride, she was expected to be in the company of a man. Too many rules. All meant to be broken.

Hightower flashed in her mind yet again. He was an arrogant prig who thought himself better than any woman, but she'd shown him she wasn't your everyday demure debutante. She was sure the man was one of those who thought women to be nothing more than property. Once the vows were said and the ink on the register barely dry, all the sweet talk disappears, and he, like the others, would change over into another version of himself. He would probably be a miserable sort of man to be married to, expecting his wife to be nothing more than someone to grace his arm in the evenings, to be a gracious hostess, and bear him an heir. And he would probably keep a mistress. He might deny it all he wanted, but men kept mistresses to ease the lack of his wife's interest in the marriage bed. Thank goodness he would be someone else's worry. The only way she would ever consider marriage would be if she fell madly in love, and he right along with her.

She urged the horse into a trot. Too many people were beginning to appear for their afternoon of see-and-be-seen. She couldn't judge too harshly. There had been a brief time when she found herself all glassy-eyed over Frederick Rivers. The man was a powerful businessman, owning a large fleet of ships that transported goods to and from exotic places like China and India.

Rivers had been a man without a title, though he had connections with some of the *ton's* wealthiest aristocrats. He had an air about him that turned people's heads, including her own. Then he revealed his true self to her one evening. It was at a ball, the Earl of Stratford's affair. She'd promised him a dance, even though he pressed her for two. After their dance they went out on the terrace like lots of other couples.

Immediately Rivers informed her of his intentions to ask her father for permission to court her, caring not that she didn't wish it. He told her she would do as he said, and then went on to presume to tell her after they married, she would reside at his country estate outside Liverpool as soon he got her with child, and if the child wasn't a boy, the process would repeat itself. He was a man to be loathed. In London she would not be allowed to leave the house without him, and if he wasn't around, she would answer to his mother, who would see to her every need. Cora had enough and fled his side. Not to be deterred, the prig had waited down the hall when she had gone to the ladies' retiring room. He forced her into an alcove in an attempt to compromise her. One swift kick with her knee into his manly parts loosened his grip on her, and cursing, he fled the scene, her opinion of the man changed forever. No man was going to own her, and certainly no man was going to have his way with her. Not without her consent. Assaulting a woman was not something gentlemen did.

Her father never asked why she refused him, but Cora was certain he had drawn his own conclusions.

7

A long line of carriages stretched for blocks, as one by one, each pulled in front of the Duke and Duchess of Liverpool's grand London home. It was, after all, the most coveted invitation of the season. To be seen at the Liverpool's annual ball meant you were among the creme of society. Everyone who was anyone was in attendance.

Lady Cora and her father descended from their carriage and were escorted to the reception line which formed in the grand hall. Quickly she scanned the elaborately painted angels which graced the ceiling. She always thought them a little too baroque for her taste, but the Duke was a powerful man, and rich and powerful men like Liverpool liked to impress others with their wealth.

Her father and the Duke of Liverpool were old friends, having met while attending Cambridge. When her mother died, the Duke and Duchess were the first to arrive at her father's side. As time passed, the Duchess always included Cora in her plans. If Cora and her father were in London, she was seen out and about, shopping with the Duchess. Having had no girls of her own, the Duchess doted on Cora.

Once she began training horses, the visits to the Liverpool country estate and shopping became less and less frequent. She always made time for the Duchess, but now, as a grown woman, she had her own life. One the Duchess would certainly not approve of.

Lady Cora held her breath as the butler announced her and her father. She walked into the crowded ballroom, eyes straight ahead.

Her father guided her toward her aunt, her mother's sister, Lady Henrietta. She wasn't a hard woman to pick out of a crowd. Once a rare beauty, her aunt's golden hair had faded, turning silver. Henrietta wasn't a tall woman, and the years had made her once trim figure into a stouter one. Cora avoided her aunt when she could, as she was constantly trying to match Cora off with a non-stop line of young men she felt suitable matches. She did the same when her brother Augustus was about, pointing out the best young ladies society had to offer. Her father tolerated his sister-in-law's meddling, telling Cora to be polite and agreeable to her aunt.

The first thing Lady Henrietta did was look at Cora's empty dance card. She shook her head. "We can't have this. You'll never find a suitable husband."

"I just arrived, my lady. No one's had a chance to sign it."

She scrutinized Cora up and down with her quizzing glass. Her aunt looked a spectacle, wearing a gown in a garish red silk, fitting far too snugly for a woman of her stature and age, but she stood solemn. "Where did you get this gown? Surely not London. I've never seen such."

Cora smoothed the skirt of the emerald-green satin moiré gown with pale yellow silk roses across her bodice and train. She smiled. "The Duchess of Liverpool's modiste made it. The pattern was one of the latest from Paris."

The mere mention of the Duchess sent her aunt sputtering and unable to respond. Viscount Lambert approached, and she forgot Cora for a moment to greet the young man.

"Viscount Lambert, I believe you've met my niece, Lady Cora?"

"I have indeed." He bent over her aunt's hand first, then turned his attention to Cora. "Lady Cora, it's been too long. You look radiant tonight."

"Thank you, my lord," she replied in a monotone. She had no interest in the Viscount and would only be polite to him because her aunt seemed to like him. He was at least twenty years her senior and hadn't aged well. Balding, portly, his face red from too much drink, which had taken its toll on the man. The rumors she'd heard were that he had gambled away most of his family fortune and was desperate to replenish his coffers.

"May I sign your dance card, Lady Cora?"

Knowing her aunt would have an apoplexy if she didn't, she reluctantly handed the card to him along with the pencil. "My lord."

A smirk crossed his face upon seeing he was the first, and immediately chose not one, but two dances to his liking. "I believe these will be adequate, my lady."

He handed her back the card. He'd penciled in the supper set and a waltz later in the evening. Rather than a large, formal sit-down dinner, the Duchess always served an elegant buffet. The Viscount would use the end of their dance to keep company during the meal.

Surely someone else had to sign her dance card.

Cora smiled politely. Her eyes were drawn to the figure approaching her. The Duke of Hightower, and for once she welcomed the mere sight of him.

"Lady Cora," he murmured, as he bent over the back of her hand. "You look lovely, as always."

Out of the corner of her eye she could see the Viscount foaming at the mouth in disbelief, and her aunt giddy at the sight of such a powerful man taking an interest in her niece.

"Your Grace."

He glanced at her dance card. "May I?"

She smiled in relief. In spite of her dislike for the man, he was going to save her from the Viscount, and that made him the better man and a gentleman. "But of course, Your Grace." She passed the card to him and watched as he studied his choices.

"May I have two dances, Lady Cora?"

"You may, Your Grace."

The edges of his mouth tugged up as he studied the card one more time. She watched as he penciled in for the first waltz and a quadrille later in the evening. He passed the dance card back to her. "I look forward to our waltz."

"As do I, Your Grace."

He bowed and took his leave. Cora watched him as he disappeared. Her nemesis was here acting as her protector. She'd seen the look in his eye as he'd seen the Viscount standing about. He didn't like it.

The Viscount also made his leave, murmuring he looked forward to their dance as well. She smiled politely as he turned and left.

"My dear, the Duke of Hightower? You'll never do better. I gather you know him?"

"Yes, we've met a couple of times," she replied without going into detail.

"He's one of the most powerful men in Parliament, you know. You would be the talk of the *ton*," Lady Turner trilled.

"I'm sure he was just being polite, Auntie, because he knows Father."

Her aunt wasn't to be deterred. "Nonsense, my dear. Did you see the way he looked at you?"

For once she was grateful to Hightower. Not only had he saved her from the Viscount's clutches, but he probably also ran off any fortune seekers from approaching her.

The music started, and before Cora realized it, it was time to dance with the Earl of Blackpool, a friend of her aunt's, who had also requested a dance.

The man was older, not the sort of Cora would have chosen for a husband. A widower, actively seeking a wife to bear him an heir, as he and his late wife had no children of their own. Luckily, the dance was a lively country dance, and she didn't have to speak with him that much. He was very gracious when he left her with her aunt, knowing she had others waiting.

She stayed with her aunt and her friends until it was time for her waltz with the Duke of Hightower. As he approached, she could feel every woman's eye on her, envious that it wasn't them.

Hightower led her to the dance floor, put one hand on her waist and took her hand in his other. As couples whirled around them, Lady Cora forgot there was a ball going on around her, her attention solely on the stunningly handsome man with whom she was dancing.

"Did I mention how exquisite you look this

evening, Lady Cora? The color is very becoming on you. It matches your eyes."

She smiled politely, hanging on his every word. "Thank you, Your Grace."

"It's a small world. I only learned this evening that the Duke and Duchess are old friends of your father's."

"Yes, they were. The Duchess and I maintain a close relationship. She was quite helpful to me after my mother died."

"Her Grace is very gracious."

"She is," Cora replied. "Now you must tell me how long you're going to be in London?"

"I head back to my country estate tomorrow. I only came for the ball. And you?"

"Same. We only came for the ball, though my father had other appointments, too. I believe we're also leaving tomorrow."

They were caught up in the music and the dance for the next few minutes. Hightower finally broke the silence.

"May I offer a word of advice, Lady Cora?"

"That depends, Your Grace."

"Look out for the Viscount. He's in desperate need of funds."

She smiled. "I heard as much. Unfortunately, I have the supper set and a waltz with him."

"That's fine, just beware of his motives," he replied.

"Thank you for your advice, Your Grace, though shouldn't I be wary of *your* motivations as well?"

"Absolutely."

"That's what I thought. Your motivation being your horse?"

"Not at all, though it couldn't hurt."

"Beware, Your Grace, of how you act. I have a lot of influence when it comes to my father."

He flashed a wicked grin. "No doubt you do. You were able to steal the Marquess's horses from right under me. Your father indulges you far too much. Has anyone told you that?"

"Only you, and I don't give a fig what you think of me, Your Grace."

His lips twitched as he tried desperately not to laugh. "As you wish," he replied. "Come, let's call a truce and enjoy the rest of our dance."

"Very well."

Hightower pulled her closer. "Would you like me to cut in at the buffet? I do outrank him." He smirked gazing into her eyes. He truly was a stunning man, with his straight nose, and square jaw, and a faint scar running along his jaw. It made him look more mysterious, as she wondered how he'd gotten it.

"I would be most grateful, Your Grace."

He nodded ever so slightly and smiled down at her. "Consider it done."

"Thank you,"

"You'll owe me for this," he replied.

"I'll *what*?" she sputtered.

"You heard me." The dance was coming to an end, and Cora wasn't going to let him off that easily.

"You're incorrigible," she hissed.

He led her off the dance floor toward her aunt. "I've been called worse."

Hightower left Cora with her aunt and walked off. Her aunt was all aglow about the possibility of having the Duke of Hightower as a member of the family.

When pigs fly. He might be on his best behavior tonight, but Cora knew his true nature. He was cunning, rude, and self-centered. Just because they were both trying to be civil, didn't mean it was anything but a show.

Viscount Lambert came for her. The supper set was a quadrille, which she hoped would keep the man at a distance. But already the man was determined to win her over. There was no doubt in her mind that Lambert would be the wrong sort of husband if she ever considered him seriously.

When the dance was over, he led her to where guests were lined up for the buffet. The Duchess went out of her way with her refreshments. She was never stingy, and the vast array of food was more than anyone would see all season.

"A delightful dance, don't you think, Lady Cora? I find quadrilles so invigorating."

She was quite certain that was true since the viscount was red-faced and out of breath. "Yes, it was."

He bent down. "May I call on you tomorrow, Lady Cora?"

Well, he certainly wasted no time getting to the point. Luckily, she had an easy way out. "I'm afraid we're headed back to Scotland tomorrow, my lord."

A flash of anger crossed his face. "Perhaps another time, then."

She nodded. "We only are in town for this event. My father would never turn it down as the Duke and Duchess are old friends of the family."

"No need to explain." He patted her hand "Another time."

Cora was getting extremely uncomfortable. The man was saying one thing to her but had something else in mind. He would go to her father, of course. Her father, though, would never force a match on her that she didn't want.

At that exact moment, just when she needed saving from this dreadful man, the Duke of Hightower appeared from out of the crowd. For once he was her guardian angel. She smiled at the sight of him. The Viscount was anything but pleased when it quickly became apparent the Duke was there for one purpose. Her.

"Your Grace," she murmured.

"I am in need of a dining partner. I thought perhaps you'd care to join me."

He was smooth, she had to credit him with that. Not even Lambert was going to object to a duke whisking away the woman he wanted to pursue. One thing about the aristocratic hierarchy—a duke outranked a mere viscount.

"I look forward to our next dance, Lady Cora," the Viscount murmured. By the stormy look in his eyes, he wasn't pleased with this turn of events.

Hightower placed her hand on his arm and led her towards the buffet line. She could feel a thousand sets of eyes watching them. It was highly unusual for Hightower to be seen with any one woman. He knew what would happen. The tongues of the *ton* would begin to wag, and suddenly she and Hightower would be paired together and married. Like that would ever happen! He was a gentleman and had just saved her from an uncomfortable situation. Nothing more.

She would pretend to enjoy his company this evening, dine and converse with him, and later dance once more. After which, hopefully, her father would be ready to leave, though he and Liverpool seemed to always have much to talk about. That was the trouble with being such intimate friends of the Duke and Duchess of Liverpool. The two men always had much to catch up on.

Perhaps her father would allow her to leave earlier. He'd brought along two footmen, so she would be well looked-after on the ride home. She could hope.

Hightower was speaking to her, and she hadn't heard a word. She simply nodded and smiled, but he was quick, knowing she wasn't paying attention. With any luck, with so many so close, he would assume it was because of the noise.

They went through the line together, choosing their meal from the huge selection the Duchess had placed out. Cora had never seen so many delectable dishes to select from.

A footman followed as Hightower found them an out-of-the-way place to eat, near an orangery the Duchess had set up for the evening, and it was less crowded than other parts of the room. Here they could converse normally, without having to raise their voices to be heard. Though what would the Duke have to say? She'd heard all she wanted to know about the man. He had a fondness for excellent horseflesh and fancied himself a breeder and owner of flat racers. There was nothing she wished to know, and small talk would be the only thing to keep her from being rude.

~

HIGHTOWER TRIED DESPERATELY NOT to smile as the footman placed their plates on a small table near the orangery. Lady Cora was doing her utmost not to have a conversation with him. True, he had been rude to her, and she should be offended. On the other hand, she was the one who'd sneaked around and had her father purchase those three horses from under him.

However, he was trying to make amends with the chit. He found her intriguing, and far more outspoken than other young ladies of his acquaintance, almost as though she was trying miserably to not like him. She was sure of herself and had no problem letting him know exactly what she was thinking.

"There," he murmured as the footman left them. "At least we can hear each other speak here."

"And why would we want to do that? There is nothing to talk about, Your Grace. Don't mistake that I would repay your having saved me from the Viscount's advances with anything other than gratitude. I have no interest in being courted by you or any other man."

Hightower snorted; his brow arched. "Court you? I can assure you, Lady Cora I have no desire to court you. In fact, you would be the last woman I would consider."

"Why's that, Your Grace? Because I speak my mind?"

"Among other things."

Her brows knit together in disapproval. "I didn't know that was bad."

"Only coming from you. Don't you agree? You can be a little overbearing." He flashed her a grin.

"You're impossible!"

He laughed. "You still didn't answer me."

"Nor will I, Your Grace."

"Hmmm, I doubt that."

"What about you, Your Grace? You're unmarried, a rake, and think because you're a duke the world owes you everything."

"Yes, I'm unmarried by my own choice. Yes, as a duke, the world around me is different. It's part of the status of being a duke. As for being a rake? That's merely a rumor. Gossip."

"You're saying there's no truth to the gossip?"

"At one point in time, maybe. My life is different

now. I have three sisters who depend on me. I cannot afford to be that sort of man."

"Very nice, Your Grace. What other fairy tales have you got?"

He knew not to be drawn into her web, so he retreated. "Let's enjoy our meal, shall we? When we are finished you can go wherever you wish, and I'll not interfere if the Viscount makes his advances again."

"You wouldn't!"

"You set the rules, my lady. You're trying your best to dislike me, and I merely rescued you from an uncomfortable situation. You should be grateful."

She shook her head. "I *am* grateful for what you've done, rescuing me from the Viscount. Truly, I am. Don't misconstrue that for anything else."

"Trust me, Lady Cora, I would never mistake what you want."

They ate in silence. He was determined to let her think she had the situation well under control. Lady Cora fascinated him in more ways than any other woman ever had.

"Do you play chess, Your Grace?" she finally asked. She put her fork down and pushed her plate to one side.

"I do on occasion," he replied. "And you, do you play, Lady Cora?"

"Yes, my father taught me. Fascinating game. I wish I were better at it."

"That can come only with practice and a variety of opponents I'm afraid. Someone who might challenge you. That's how you get better playing the game."

"When was the last time you played, Your Grace?"

He thought for a moment before answering. "Sadly, it's been a while."

"Pity. You really need to practice," she replied. "You know practice makes perfect."

"I'm sure it does, Lady Cora. I'm sure you view life as one huge chess game. In fact I'm positive you're playing a game of chess right now." She remained silent, but not before he caught a brief smile flash across her face. Indeed this was all one huge game to her. One she felt she excelled at. In time he would prove her wrong.

He noticed she'd been pushing her food about her plate. She'd eaten very little. He himself finished and sat back for a footman to take the plate away. Lady Cora nodded to the young man to remove hers as well.

"I'm not overly fond of rich sauces," she remarked.

"I'm sure you could have another plate brought if you'd like. Without the sauce of course," he replied. "I'd be happy to wait for you to finish."

"No, that's not necessary, Your Grace."

"Perhaps you'd care to go outside and get some fresh air?"

She nodded. "Yes, it is rather warm in here."

He led her to the open French doors. There were couples strolling along the long terrace, some in the garden below enjoying the delightful weather. Torches lit the pathway as couples walked leisurely. Hightower knew not to even suggest walking the gardens to her. She was suspicious and would immediately take him for having an alternative motive.

They walked across the width of the terrace to the balustrade. At least they could look down at the gardens and have some sense of privacy, thought it was hard with the crush that had been invited. People seemed to be everywhere.

"It's a beautiful evening," he said.

"Yes, it is, though it still is London."

"No denying that. The sky is not nearly as clear as it is in the country. The smoke from the factories have ruined our skies," he replied quietly.

"Have you ever been to Scotland, Your Grace? The sky is clear. You can see every star in the sky."

He turned toward her, looking down at her. His lips curved slightly at the sight of her in her finest gown. "Yes, I've been to Scotland a time or two. You're right, the sky is magnificent at night. Nothing can compare."

The strains of music could be heard coming from inside as the musicians prepared for the next set of dancing. No one out on the terrace seemed in any hurry to go back inside.

"Shall I return you to your aunt?" he finally asked.

She sighed and nodded. "Yes, I suppose you must, or she'll make something out of what she will deem as 'spending a good amount of time together.'"

"Yes, and we couldn't have that, could we?"

"No, because she'll have us married off by the end of the evening," she replied. "If not you, she'll find someone else. My aunt thinks I need to be looking for a husband."

"And aren't you?"

"No," she replied firmly. "I don't have the time for marriage or a husband. I doubt there's any man alive I would even consider. And you, Your Grace? Is there a reason you've not married?"

"Like you, I haven't the time nor have I found the perfect duchess yet."

"Pity."

"Why's that?"

"Because every mother and most all the young

ladies here are frothing at the mouth like wild beasts, wanting to win your favor?" she asked.

"Then I'm afraid they'll all be disappointed." He turned and extended his arm. She smiled and placed her hand on it. "Shall we?"

"If we must," she sighed.

"Don't sound so enthusiastic, Lady Cora."

"I just hate all this, that's all."

He nodded and patted her hand. "I understand, trust me."

She cocked her head and peered up at him. She licked her lips, the sight of which almost rendered Hightower weak-kneed. "I believe you do."

He led her back indoors and through the crowd, until they found her aunt sitting to one side of the ballroom with a couple of other matronly older women.

"I look forward to our next dance, Lady Cora."

"As do I, Your Grace, and thank you for keeping me company."

He bowed. "You're most welcome, Lady Cora." He turned to her aunt and her friends who were watching with great interest. "Ladies."

Lady Cora had his emotions going in more different directions than he was comfortable with. One moment he had contempt for her, the next he was warming up to her. Why couldn't she just be like any other woman who couldn't think for herself?

Instead she was an independent, free-thinking young woman, who kept drawing him into her web, but the moment she saw he had the slightest spark of interest, she froze him out.

He'd done well this evening, too. He hadn't even brought up her trainer, nor sending Apollo to him.

She'd made it quite clear the last time they spoke on the matter that he would have to wait. And wait he would.

As he walked the perimeter, he noted his friend Allgood motioning for him to come join him. He was a welcome sight. The sooner he was out of this room, the better. It was stifling, not only from all the bodies, but knowing so many eyes were on him. Mothers and their daughters.

"You look as if you could use a drink," Allgood said dryly as he approached his friend.

"That is the best thing anyone has said to me all evening."

Allgood clapped him on the shoulder and smiled. "Come, the Duke has a card room set up with a rather well-stocked bar."

"Lead the way," Hightower replied.

"I saw you with Lady Cora. For disliking the chit, you certainly are spending time with her."

"You read into things far more than you should. Viscount Lambert is trying to worm his way into her affections. Lady Cora has excellent intuition. She saw right through Lambert, but you know the Viscount. He's desperate for a wife with a large dowry."

"So, you played the knight in shining armor and came to her rescue?"

Hightower's lips curled upward. "Yes, I suppose you can say I did."

"How chivalrous of you. I'm surprised she didn't toss you out as well, given the dislike she seems to have for you," Allgood replied.

"I believe she guards her emotions closely."

"She's been hurt before. That's understandable if that's the case." Allgood said solemnly.

Hightower wasn't so sure what to make of Lady

Cora. Something told him her tough exterior was armor to something more fragile. He wasn't sure he wanted to pursue the matter. Saving her from men with not-so-nice intentions was enough, at least for now.

8

Early the next morning, Hightower rose early for one last ride in the park. He enjoyed riding along the Serpentine in the early morning hours. The only people present this time of day were nannies with their charges, or merchants making their way through. Anyone else rarely rose before late morning. He always loved Hyde Park before the crowds descended on it and the tranquility turned into a social scene where members of the ton went to be seen. He could gallop his horse with ease, without fear of having to rein the animal in because of crowds or the occasional ill-mannered rider. Sometimes on these morning rides he would find himself a quiet place to sit and contemplate his day, or he brought a book along to read. This was his one way to escape the demands of the Dukedom while in London.

Hightower rode to a favorite place of his along the Serpentine. As he did, he noted a familiar figure bending over their mount as though removing a stone or checking for perhaps a loose shoe. No, it couldn't possibly be. Of all the people and places in London, what were the odds of running into Lady Cora. Where was her groom? Surely, she hadn't ridden out alone.

No, she would. She was just daring enough to sneak into her father's mews and saddle her own horse before any of the grooms knew she'd left.

He neared, dismounting his own horse, trying his best not to notice the fact that Lady Cora was dressed in breeches. Dear God, dressed in tight breeches, riding through Hyde Park. Breeches which showed off the curve of her round bottom and hips. What was she thinking? Better yet, what was she up to?

"Lady Cora, good morning. Where is your groom? He should be better suited to remove a stone from your horse's shoe."

She peered up at him with a hard look on her face. "I'm perfectly capable of taking care of my own mount. My groom is nowhere to be found because I left him at the entrance to the park."

He grew closer. "Here, at least let me have a look."

"Your Grace, I am not some fragile young debutante who can barely ride sidesaddle."

He held up his hands in mock defeat. "Very well."

She sighed, putting the animal's leg down, but holding up a small pebble triumphantly in her fingers. "You see? I only require a groom because society dictates it. I'm perfectly able to take care of myself while riding in the park or anywhere else."

"So you've made abundantly clear. May I ask why you are out so early in the morning? And dressed like that?" The words flew out of his mouth before he could stop them. It was true.

There was a flash in those green eyes, daring him. "You don't approve of my dress, Your Grace? Not that I care. In fact, I rather love that you disapprove," she said sarcastically.

He made a low sound deep in his throat. "I, um, just find it unusual. That's all."

"I ride like this all the time," she replied with a grin. "Don't worry, my father is well aware of my preference."

He nodded, unsure what to say. She had a quick tongue and held nothing back. Not a favorable trait for a lady, but none the less he found it intriguing. She was most affable and in spite of her wicked tongue, was easy to converse with. Finally, he broke the awkward silence.

"Would you care to walk for a while, or do you have somewhere to be?"

"No, I have nowhere to be. We're taking the train back to Scotland in the morning. My father had some last-minute business he had to tend to."

"I see," he replied. He began to lead his horse along the path in front of the Serpentine, somehow knowing she would accompany him.

"And you, Your Grace?"

He shook his head. "I leave this afternoon for my estate."

She shrugged. "I see. Decided for one last ride before heading home?" she asked. "I'm surprised to see you out this early."

"I've always enjoyed riding here early in the day. This is one of my favorite areas, and for your information, I always arise early." They continued to walk side-by-side. Hightower tried his best not to look down at her. Seeing her bottom hugging those breeches gave him a cockstand. And where that came from, he had no idea, but it scared the hell out of him.

She stopped and peered up at him as though to say something. His composure would allow no more. He lowered his head, cupped her face with large hands, and kissed her. The kiss was full of passion as his tongue explored the depths of her mouth. She kissed him back, pressing her body against his. Her lips were warm, her tongue daring to play with his. He tore his mouth from hers, and their eyes met. What he saw confused him. She didn't appear to *not* like what they had just shared, but he instinctively knew she wasn't overjoyed with succumbing to her needs.

"I apologize, that was unforgivable on my part. It wasn't the act of a gentleman."

"My goodness, Hightower! It was just an innocent kiss," she replied with a smirk.

"Is that what you think? That it was simply an innocent kiss?"

"Of course. You read too much into it."

He bent down and spoke lowly. "Did I? Do you know what you do to me and what I'd like for us to share?"

"Don't think a man hasn't spoken of such to me before."

"You're playing a dangerous game, Lady Cora. You do know what might happen if it were another man? One with less self-control than I have?"

She rolled her eyes. "No one is ever going to try and take advantage of me. I can take care of myself. You overreact, Your Grace."

"Do I? What about a certain viscount who was fawning over you? Do you really think he wouldn't compromise you in a heartbeat to gain your dowry?"

"As I said, you're making a big fuss over nothing. Every man in my acquaintance is a gentleman. Except perhaps you, and I usually try and never spend time with a rake."

"Don't call me that. We've been over the matter. Leave it alone." He could spar with her all day long when it came to words, but he drew the limit. She was baiting him, trying to fluster him into saying something he might regret.

She sighed. "Very well. We're finished—for now."

He nodded. "Thank you."

"I do need to find my groom. I'm sure he's at the entrance, frantic that I duped him once again."

He nodded. "Yes, of course."

"Would you mind holding his bridle while I mount?"

He nodded and watched as she swung her leg over the gelding's back. He tried not to look too closely, especially right now.

"Thank you for your help, Your Grace, and for the walk, as short as it was. Good day to you."

"Lady Cora. I look forward to our next encounter," he replied.

"I'm sure you do," she laughed, turning her horse and galloping away from him.

He stood watching her as she disappeared. His face twitched. Why in the hell had he kissed her? What was he trying to prove? He recalled how she responded to him, and had no doubt if she had disliked it, she would have ended it immediately, most likely with a slap to his face. But she hadn't. She seemed to enjoy it almost as much as he did.

Hightower shook his head. It wouldn't surprise him at all if she had had an alternative motive for allowing him to kiss her, or even for daring to respond to him.

He smiled as he mounted his gelding. Reading would have to wait. He was too distracted right now, thanks to Lady Cora.

He had to admit, she was an exquisite creature.

Sebastian smiled, wondering how Lady Cora would act when next the two met.

~

Cora urged her horse back toward the park's entrance, knowing her groom would be waiting. He had been subject to her deliberate and willful acts before. They had an understanding; he let her ride as she pleased in the park, and he enjoyed a position as her personal groom. The only time he accompanied her was when her father, or someone he insisted she ride with was with her. Otherwise, he left her to her own devices.

What had she been thinking?

She had been kissed before, always in private, never in the middle of a public park. She kissed the others out of curiosity. The kiss she just shared with His Grace was unlike any other she'd experienced. He had leisurely explored the depth of her mouth with his tongue, then lazily ran it across the seam of her mouth, leaving her dazed with long, drugging kisses.

Cora had never been kissed with passion like this. Hightower had held her intentionally close, making her aware of the subtle movements of his body, his possessive touch. Besides riding horses and working in her stables, she found another reason wearing breeches had such freedom. She would have never felt his touch nearly as well if she'd been attired in a dress, corset, and the layers a woman was deemed to wear.

She never imagined the man's kiss would have her heart racing and make her want more. She'd swayed closer, wanting to feel all there was to the man.

A smile tugged at the corners of her mouth as she realized her lips were swollen. Bloody hell, but she'd like to do that with him again.

No! She wouldn't allow herself to be taken in by his ploy. She couldn't let him try and distract her. All he wanted was to send his stallion for training. Was this an attempt to change her mind? Did he really think sharing one kiss might possibly change her mind? If he thought to humiliate her into subjection, he was sadly mistaken.

He'd figured out how much influence he thought she had over her father when it came to horses that were taken in for training. Hightower thought he could win her over by toying with her affections. She would have to be on her top of her game the next time they met. Next time she wouldn't lose her head over a handsome, brooding, willful duke.

Nearing the park's entrance, she easily found Edward, her groom, waiting patiently on his dark bay. She nodded to him, letting him know they'd be leaving. They rarely spoke during these rides. Edward had been with her long enough, was good with the horses, and had a keen interest in learning more about their care and training.

Cora thought she was in the clear as she and Edward left the park. Part of the reason she enjoyed her rides this early. Few were out and about. This time she had been caught—again.

"Cora, is that you?" she heard a familiar voice call out to her.

She brought her gelding to a halt and peered to her right as Lady Betsy Armstrong came trotting up. She was riding sidesaddle, and Cora almost couldn't help but smile as her friend observed her attire.

"You're out rather early, Betsy."

"True, but it's the best time to escape my mother and grandmother's grand plans. At least for an hour or two," she replied. Betsy was the exact opposite of Cora. Pale blond and petite, in comparison to Cora's height and dark hair.

"Though I wouldn't think they arise before noon, do they?"

Betsy shook her head. "Not when there's an afternoon of shopping involved. I'll barely have time to change when I return."

"I didn't know you were in town," Cora said. "I hadn't seen you until now."

"I know. Not that I've been avoiding you or anyone else. It's just that I'm being courted by the Marquess of Northwood, and he keeps me busy taking me places I've never been to in London, like Greenwich. We had a picnic there. It was so delightful. He also took me to the National Museum, which I adore. Oh, and I almost forgot. We've been to see the hot air balloons twice."

"He must like you a lot, and judging from the look on your face, I have to say you care a great deal for this young man as well."

"I do!" Betsy exclaimed. "Mother says it's just a matter of time before he and I are betrothed."

"I'm happy for you," she replied. "We'll have to get together next time we're both in town, or if your family ventures north to Scotland." She was happy for her friend, realizing her friends would soon be married with new lives, and she would be, by her own choice, alone. Cora, however, had more. She had her freedom and choice to make her own decisions.

"Are you here long?"

Cora smiled gently. "No. Papa had some business matters to tend to before we can leave."

Betsy furled her brow. "The Marquess is coming for tea later, after we return from shopping. Perhaps next time?"

"Of course," she said. "In the meantime, you must

write me and tell me all about this young man. I look forward to meeting him."

"I shall," she said, looking down at Cora's breeches, arching a brow. "Does your father know you ride astride and in breeches here?"

"Of course, he does. Shocking, I know."

"Is there anyone special in your life?"

Cora smiled and shook her head. "No, but I'm fine with the idea of being put on the shelf. I have too many things going on at our estate in Scotland to be tied down right now."

"You must tell me all about them. I hate it, but I need to go."

"But of course. I need to see to a few things myself," Cora replied awkwardly.

Betsy had been the closest thing to a sister Cora had ever had. The two of them spent a lot of summers together in Scotland, and when in London, they were inseparable. That all changed once they both had their coming out. Betsy became obsessed with the young men and was determined to find the perfect husband of rank and status. Cora hoped her friend had found it in Northwood.

She turned her horse back around and continued her walk back home. Shaking her head, she wondered how long it might be before she heard her friend was betrothed. Clandestine, secret meetings just wasn't something Betsy normally did. She did everything as she'd been raised, which made her wonder about the Marquess of Northwood. Cora couldn't recall him, but she so rarely attended a lot of social events when in London, that didn't surprise her. She would ask her father if he'd heard of him.

When she finally rode up to the mews behind the family London home, she quickly dismounted and handed the reins to her groom, after patting the gelding and giving him the carrot she kept in her pocket. Walking through the gate and garden, Cora made her way to the kitchen door. It was far easier to enter here than chance going through the drawing room and finding her father with colleagues.

Entering the kitchen she scurried through so as not to startle some of the kitchen maids by her presence. Though some of the older women had seen her dressed in breeches before, it still startled the younger ones. Cora had almost made it to the back staircase when she was confronted by the butler. He always did his best not to let it show he thought her riding attire was inappropriate for a young woman of her breeding.

"Your father sent word that he has arranged for both of you to return to Scotland on the late train this evening."

That was wonderful news to Cora. The sooner she could get back to her beloved horses the better. "Thank you. Did he say anything else?"

"No, my lady, that was all." He looked down his hawk nose at her like he always did. Apart from his dislike of her attire, Cora and he rubbed along. He'd been with the family for years, his older brother the butler at their Scottish estate.

"Excellent. Would you have Cook prepare some toast and eggs? Have them served in the breakfast room. I'll be down in an hour."

He nodded. "As you wish, my lady."

Cora turned and headed up the back stairs to her rooms. She would take a quick bath and dress before having her late breakfast. Afterwards she would make sure her lady's maid was started on packing. This afternoon, while she waited on her father's return, she would tend to the correspondence she received since being in London. She made note to send a letter to Betsy. She wanted to find out exactly what was going on with her friend.

She smiled. They would be back home in Scotland by early morning. Nothing outside of her horses could make her happier. Her mind, however, quickly flashed to Hightower and their earlier encounter. Surely something as innocent as that kiss wasn't going to keep invading her very thoughts, no matter how much she had enjoyed it.

The weather forced Sebastian to ride in his carriage rather than ride his horse. Rotten English weather—one minute it might be gray and pouring down rain, the next sunny and bright. He loathed the confined space of a carriage. It gave him too much time to think. Fortunately, Hightower Hall was close enough to London he could make the journey in a day. With the weather such as it was, it would take longer. Roads would become muddy and slick before long, but they would press on until they arrived in Warwickshire. The idea of spending the night at an inn when they were so close was not an option. He needed to be home tending to his estate and getting an update on how Apollo's Gold was liking his newfound holiday.

Surprisingly, Sebastian found himself missing the young colt. The two shared a bond, but every time he left the colt behind at Hightower Hall, he had to remind himself that the stallion was a racer, and when he retired, he would breed what Sebastian hoped would be magnificent, fast youngsters.

He shut the curtains in hopes that he might be

able to sleep an hour or so. After his encounter with Lady Cora, Sebastian found himself able to concentrate on little else. He couldn't keep her out of his thoughts.

Leaning back against the squabs, Sebastian closed his eyes and hoped the lull of the carriage would help him fall fast asleep. Sleep, however, wasn't his, this dreary day. He picked a novel he'd purchased in London. Opening the book, he leaned over and reopened the curtains on the side closest to him.

Once again, he found himself unable to concentrate. Lady Cora and Apollo kept slipping onto the pages. He shut the book and stared at the curtains until his body succumbed to much needed sleep.

He awakened to the change in the movement of the carriage as it slowed and turned. He glanced out the window. Hightower Hall stood at the end of the oak-lined drive in all its glory. Probably for the best on such a dreary day, as his dreams were filled with Lady Cora, and that disturbed him.

He was home and had many things to occupy his mind or that required his attention. Though he had a competent estate manager, he liked to stay on top of everything, making sure to have regular meetings with his man, in between going over all estate ledgers himself monthly. The estate was making good money, and he had no intention of sliding backwards.

James, his longtime butler, stood at the top of the steps as he descended from the carriage. The man was efficient. How he knew the precise time of his arrival had always mystified Sebastian. Either the man spent a lot of his time looking out windows at the front of the house, or he had some young boy placed somewhere watching for him.

Sebastian took the steps two at a time, handing the hawknosed butler his hat as he passed into the grand entry.

"Everything as it should be?" he inquired.

"Yes, Your Grace."

"Excellent. I'm going to the stables first. When I return, I'll take a bath and change. I'll have dinner in my study this evening while I catch up on my correspondence."

The man bowed slightly, like he always did. "As you wish Your Grace."

Sebastian pulled his greatcoat closed, handed James his gloves, and made his way to the back door leading out to the stables. He ran through the downpour, which hadn't let up since he left London. He quickly made it to the stables where he immediately heard a familiar nicker. Sebastian headed to the stallion's stall, opened the door and entered. He began to stroke the chestnut's neck and talk lowly to him.

No one was around. There wouldn't be until a bit later, when one of the grooms or the stablemaster made a final check. One of the young grooms usually slept in the stables as a precaution, in case of illness or whatever else might occur. For now, it was him and the soft munching of horses chewing their hay.

He spent fifteen minutes or so softly talking to the stallion before leaving him. Tomorrow he'd make a point of observing him out in his pasture. See how he was getting along with his temporary new-found freedom.

Returning to the house, he quickly made his way up the stairs to his rooms. He stripped off his clothes, tossing them on a chair before stepping into the bath his majordomo had prepared moments earlier.

Adding interior water pipes, both hot and cold had been one of the best investments he'd made to the old home.

Sebastian lowered himself into the steaming tub, his head against the back as his body relaxed. At least for a few minutes. He found himself in a fury of emotions. All because he'd kissed Lady Cora. One minute he detested himself for what he'd done, the next with a cockstand as none he'd ever experienced. One that would not go away, no matter how hard he tried.

That kiss. Bloody hell. He'd completely lost control, letting lust overcome him. Not an emotion he submitted to. Not with someone like Lady Cora.

It had been a good thing they'd been in a public place, because given a little more time and he would have lost his head. That wasn't the sort of man he was anymore.

He sat up and shook his head, reaching for a cake of wintergreen soap. He ran the bar over his chest and arms. He wondered what Lady Cora would think of his body. Some women had a disdain for men's physiques, while others embraced the male species. Which was she? He imagined her being bossy, wanting more. He never left a woman unsatisfied, and Lady Cora would be well sated by the time he finished with her.

Where had that come from?

He took the cake of soap and washed his hair. Sinking under the water, he rinsed his hair. He needed to dress and ready himself for dinner and an evening in his study.

An image of her overtook him. He groaned and slid back into the water and took hold of his cock. Minutes later the orgasm tore through him like a blazing fire. His body convulsed. This would never do, nor could it replace the real woman.

Thirty minutes later, he made his way downstairs and to his study. He poured himself a brandy before sitting behind the massive oak desk, which had been in service to many generations of dukes. Swirling the brandy, he took a sip. Setting the glass aside, he began to go through correspondence that had accumulated over his time away.

Some time later, James and a footman entered with a cart, his dinner on top. A good place to stop, especially since his mind kept wandering elsewhere.

SEBASTIAN FOUND himself in a much better mood the following morning as he headed downstairs. The sun was shining, though it was peeking in and out of clouds. A perfect time to take his usual morning ride. Today he'd take a young piebald gelding he recently acquired for Matilda. She had yet to ride the youngster, because he wanted to make sure the horse was sound and sufficiently trained before he let her loose on it.

Walking to the stables, he noticed Apollo already out in his pasture, kicking up his heels and running as though there were no tomorrow. If he could only get the stallion to use his speed on a track again, he would be relieved. He stopped to watch, pleased with his decision to give the creature some time off.

The stables were abuzz with the usual morning activities. He found one of the grooms finishing up with the piebald. He thanked the young man and led the gelding outside. Sebastian rechecked the girth and bridle before swinging his leg over the gelding's back. Gathering the reins, he urged youngster on.

He headed toward a large empty field that led to the east side of the estate. There had been a problem with one of the rock walls separating the Marquess of Wiltshire's estate from Hightower Hall. Age and some bad workmanship had caused a portion of the wall to crumble. Wiltshire had been insistent that it was Sebastian's responsibility to fix since his ancestors had built it. Not one wishing to stir up problems, Sebastian took the repair to hand.

As he was on his way to the wall, Sebastian noted at how well maintained the estate was. Having ridden on the fringes of the orchard, he was pleased how well the apple trees were looking. His estate manager, Cooper, had hired someone whose job was to maintain the orchards. See that they produced well, that the trees were free of rot and insects, and anything else that plagued these fragile trees.

The apple orchard alone produced enough apples for not only the house, but for his tenants as well. Nothing went to waste. Quite the change from when his father had controlled the estate. His interests were never in estate management—that was for others to deal with. Unlike Sebastian's view towards the estate, his father saw himself as a duke, and such matters were beneath him. Sebastian had had his moments; he knew that. Once, when he first became duke, he felt the same as his father, but as he grew more comfortable into the role for which he'd been trained his whole life, he found he could do so much more.

He reined the gelding in as he neared the new portion of wall, noting the men had done an excellent job rebuilding the crumbled section. All the rocks which had been in place for years had been cleaned and reused to close the hole in the wall.

Satisfied, he rode off. His next stop was one of his favorite places. It was one spot on the entire estate he could be left alone and in peace. It had given him peace from his father and the outside world. Situated at the top of a small hill, it was surrounded by trees as it looked down at the estate. No one came here, because it was left alone for the deer and other animals that roamed the estate. He would come here as a young boy, to read or just take a break from his tutors. All an important part of molding him into the future duke.

Sebastian had recently shared the spot with his estate manager, asking that a portion of it be cleared. He'd requested a bench be placed far enough back that it couldn't be seen, so that he might be able to come and sit or enjoy a picnic away from prying eyes.

As he rode, his mind wandered to Lady Cora. He wondered how she felt about picnics, and if she would enjoy herself there. Bloody hell, what was he doing thinking about that woman! She was the one thing blocking his being able to send Apollo to her father's trainer, and she seemed determined to see that it never happened. She was meddlesome, poking her nose into things women had no business in.

He was almost there when Cooper, his estate manager, came riding up. They were supposed to meet, but that was later and in his study. He wondered if something was amiss, or if the man simply wanted to accompany him, as he did so often. Sebastian found the man far more competent than most when it came to running the estate, and they shared the same interests in future plans for the land and people working it. The world was changing. Estates were no longer a main source of income for peers as they had once been, and new uses for the land and outside investments were needed to keep income flowing.

"Cooper. Did I misunderstand you? I thought we were to meet in my study later."

The black-haired man shook his head as he joined Sebastian. "We are, but I thought I might join you. Unless of course, His Grace would rather ride alone."

"No, I just checked out the wall that has been re-built, and I was on my way to the hill."

"Was the wall to His Grace's satisfaction?" Cooper inquired as they began to walk their horses side-by-side.

"Yes, very well done. Now if it would only keep Wiltshire and his drunken guests out, I would indeed be happy," Sebastian replied with a smile.

Cooper sighed. "One can only hope, Your Grace."

Sebastian arched a brow and looked at the man. "I really don't want to have to be seen as the unfriendly neighbor, but I want to know next time he and his guests trespass. I don't want to, but if need be, I'll send him a strongly worded letter, asking him to keep his hunts and such to his property. It isn't like he doesn't have plenty of land."

"I'll keep an eye out for signs of the Marquess and his parties. It shouldn't be too hard, as I have men working nearby on reseeding the pasture near there as you requested."

He nodded. "Good, because I would be most un-happy if they were to trample everything your men have worked so hard at."

"Consider it taken care of, Your Grace. Would you like to see the hill, and what's been done there?"

"Yes," Sebastian replied. "It's still hidden from view? No one can see it just by looking up at the hill?"

"Yes, Your Grace, it's still well hidden, and no one will know it is there. We simply cleaned it up and made it more habitable for you to spend quiet time."

"I appreciate that, Cooper," he replied. "Come, let's give these beasts a good gallop."

With that, Sebastian headed off across the meadow and toward his hill.

10

"I have sent word to the Duke of Hightower inviting him to send his stallion for training at the end of the month," the Duke of Dover said, as he picked up a piece of buttered toast, and his gaze shifted across the table to Cora.

It was two days after Cora and her father had arrived back at the family estate in Scotland. Cora had stayed busy working with the horses she had in training. As her father usually stayed out of what horses she chose to take on, this was a huge blow to Cora.

She looked across the table at him. "Very well, though I protest not being consulted on this beforehand."

"I told him you, or should I say *our trainer*, would be in touch shortly to discuss details."

Cora shook her head. "I'm not entirely sure I'll be ready for his horse by then."

The edges of the Duke's mouth pulled upward. "I think you protest far too much where Hightower is concerned."

"The man is impossible. He's arrogant and thinks far too much of himself and that stallion of his," she shot back.

"You're entitled to your opinions, but I've invited him to send his horse for training as we agreed, and you will oblige me."

Cora sat back in her chair and studied her father closely. "Don't think I don't know what you're up to. You're trying to make a match for me with Hightower."

"What if I am? It's past time you married, Cora. You could do no better than Hightower."

"When donkeys fly!" she shot back, her dark green eyes ablaze. What was he up to? Had Hightower talked with him, expressing an interest in her?

"You've scared off every man in the land who shows an interest, Cora. I think Hightower is attracted to you, and this would be a perfect opportunity for the two of you to get to know each other."

"Surely he won't have time to accompany his stallion."

Again, the Duke smiled at his daughter. "I invited him to come stay a fortnight to see his horse settled in."

"How am I supposed to train my other clients' horses with him here?"

"By the time Hightower arrives, all your other clients' animals will have departed. Simply tell him our trainer is away with other horses," the Duke replied. "Sooner or later, when you find a young man to marry, you're going to have to share your secret."

"Hightower is the last man I'd ever marry!"

The Duke pushed back his chair and rose with a smile. "I'll be in my study if you need me."

"I won't. I'm going to the stables. I have two clients' horses which need my attention if they're to depart before the Duke's esteemed stallion arrives," she replied sarcastically.

Her father shook his head of graying hair and

walked toward the door, ignoring her comments. He was still a handsome man, and why he had never re-married Cora never understood. He had never pushed either her brother Augustus or her to marry, always saying they would each know when they found the right person. Why he was changing his mind now was quite curious to Cora. But Hightower? Never!

Once her father left, Cora pushed back her chair and left the breakfast room. She needed to temper her anger before she got to the stables. Horses were sensitive, and acutely aware of those around them. She walked out of the house and slowly made her way to the stables, stopping to admire some roses which had bloomed in the small garden in front of the house. Her mother had them planted there, saying it was a shame to waste the round, grass-filled space, which only had borne a statue of a lion. Her grandfather had built it and added the statue. She couldn't recall why he chose a lion, but it had always seemed fitting.

Walking the pathway leading to the stables, she looked out at the new stallion she'd recently gotten. He was standing near the fence watching her, his ears up and at attention. The stables had long been her favorite place to come, ever since she was a child. Any excuse she could find, she would bolt from the endless piano practices, tutoring, and needlework in exchange for being near her beloved horses. Even as a girl, she had considered them all hers. Cora didn't need to ride —just being near them made her relax and enjoy her day. Her mother never approved of her devotion to the horses and the stables and tried to keep her daughter close. The Duke on the other hand, was aware of the attraction, as he himself loved nothing better than to ride across his vast estate, sometimes with Cora.

Try as she might to keep Hightower and what her

father had told her at breakfast out of her thoughts, it kept replaying in her mind. This was not the time for such foolishness. She would write Hightower herself, telling him there was no need to come, just send his horse with a trusted groom. She would contact him when the stallion had made significant progress. She didn't need his ill-mannered, arrogant person here. He would want to know everything, and she didn't want to have to explain about anything her "trainer" might undertake with his horse.

She also knew better than to protest too much in front of her father, especially since he seemed to have this notion that she needed to marry and thought Hightower to be a decent choice. She would say nothing and try to be pleasant whenever the Duke was mentioned, for now. If things changed, she would make her own choice. No one was going to make her marry such a vile man. Not even her father.

CORA WAS STANDING in the middle of one of the small paddocks, working one of the youngsters in her charge on the lunge line. The gray filly was coming along nicely, and Cora had hopes to begin taking the youngster out onto the track under saddle in the next day or so. With any luck, Temptress would be ready for her to be returned to her owner in Surrey for the owner's local trainer to enter her into her first race. She startled at a familiar disapproving voice behind her. Augustus.

"I see some things never change, Sister."

She whirled around to see Augustus leaning on the fence watching her. He looked older, more muscular than the last time she'd seen him. His inky black hair hung just over his collar, his glass-green eyes closely watching her.

Ignoring his biting remark, she responded, just not the way he would expect. Augustus would expect her to lash out at him, but she was not going to fall into his trap.

"Augustus! When did you return?" she asked, as she gathered the line and led the mare towards him. "Papa hadn't said anything about your return."

"Just now, though I will admit I landed in Edinburgh a week ago. I went to see friends while there. Papa didn't know because I hadn't written him with my return plans," he replied.

"So, what now?"

"In good time. There is still much for Papa and me to catch up on."

She patted the filly and handed her off to a groom as she walked out of the paddock. "Good, I know he's missed your input, and I'm glad you won't be living far away."

"He says you have no prospects for marriage, and refuse any and all suggestions," he said. "It's past time you gave up this nonsense and married."

Cora arched a brow. "When I'm ready to marry, I'm sure I won't have any problem finding a worthy man."

"That's where you're wrong, Sister. You're already considered on the shelf by some. Father has agreed to my inviting a couple of bachelor friends of mine from University who are on the marriage mart. I think one of the two should suit."

"I will not be coerced into a marriage I have no desire for," she spat out. "You're no better than Papa."

"He's only doing what's best for you, as am I."

"I'm much too busy, and the answer is no."

He gestured with his hand. "All of this nonsense?

It can be taken away from you as easily as it was allowed. Papa has an excellent man who runs the stables and breeding program already in place. He can find another trainer for the racers. No, it is time to give this up, Cora. Time for you to marry and act like the lady you were brought up to be."

Cora closed the space between them, poking him in the chest with her finger. "I have clients."

"You will honor what you've committed to, but will take on no more," he replied, his eyes darkening. Augustus did not like to be confronted or told how to act. Never had.

"I don't take orders from you, and for your information this is *my* business!"

"On this matter you will do as I say. Papa and I agree, and he's allowing me to finish it."

"The hell he is! And what of your own estate?"

"What of it? It's a mere five miles from here. My estate manager has kept everything running smoothly while I've been away," he replied. "Mark my words, Sister, you *will* comply and submit to this change. You will find a suitable husband by the end of summer, or one will be chosen for you."

"Go to Hell!" she spat out, as she spun around on her heel and quickly walked toward the stable. The best action for her now would be to ignore him. Avoid the subject at any cost, with either her father or Augustus. She had enough horses in training for at least another two months.

If her father had written Hightower about sending his stallion, she could make excuses and keep him here for further training, and that might take her through the autumn. She needed to send word to the Duke as well. She didn't need her brother ruining everything for her, and that's exactly what Augustus would do if given the chance. She pitied the woman he married. His expectations were so high for her, that anyone he chose to marry would have to be flawless. She would come from a very well-to-do family, have a spotless reputation, would have to be a beauty. Augustus never had been seen in the company of women who weren't beauties. Finally, she would bear him at least an heir and a spare, and probably a lot more. She wondered if he had someone in mind, or if he was still the rake she'd understood him to be.

Unfortunately for Cora, her brother followed her to the stables. He always had to have the last word. Why should he be any different after two years?

"I need a list of the horses you've taken in, when they'll be finished and how many more you have committed to," he muttered.

"This is my domain, Brother. I do not answer to you, only Papa."

"And as I told you, I'm taking over. You've been coddled too long, and it ends now," he replied sternly.

"I'm sorry, Augustus. I have a full schedule, so if there's nothing more, I would like to get back to my clients' horses," she said, "And I don't answer to you. You have no say in what I do here."

"As you wish, but this isn't over, Cora."

She folded her arms. "I can see your trip did nothing to improve your disposition. You're still the same—an older version, but as horrid as ever. I pity you, Brother. You're going to become a bitter old man if you don't change your ways."

"Don't try and change the subject and turn this into all about me."

Again she turned and walked away from him. Thank goodness women's rights were changing. She could now own her own land, have her own money, her own successful business. She knew if anything happened to their father, when it finally did, Augustus would have her out by her ear. Her father had provisions for her in addition to her own holdings. Unfortunately, her brother would be the one controlling the purse strings, and regardless of what their father wished, he would do as he pleased. Augustus would be shocked when he learned how much she obtained on her own.

11

Cora watched from afar as the Duke of Hightower's carriage approached her home. Behind his carriage was an enclosed wagon transporting his stallion. Blast him! Why had he insisted on accompanying the animal and seeing him settled? Her father had graciously helped her cause by informing Hightower their resident trainer would not be on hand when Apollo's Gold arrived, telling the Duke in their correspondence the man had accompanied a pair he'd trained to the west isles of Scotland and wouldn't return for at least a fortnight. Hopefully, that would entice the Duke to head back to his own estate or London, and not stay.

Her other concern was Augustus. He showed up every couple of days unannounced either to go over business matters with their father, or to watch her, taunt her. He would simply stand and watch her as she took various horses through their training. Never saying a word, just a smirk she would love to slap off his face. She refused to speak with him on anything to do with the stables, as she was afraid of antagonizing him or have him go running to their father with some made-up allegation as to why she needed to be married.

Augustus hadn't shown up today, probably because his friends were in residence. She imagined the three bachelors, all too busy drinking, smoking cheroots, and scheming. Hopefully too busy to introduce her to either of them, but she knew better. Her brother was on a mission to see her married, and the sooner the better.

She decided to stay away from the stables when Hightower's stallion arrived. She didn't want to have to speak with the Duke right now and didn't want him thinking she spent her spare time at the stables. Instead, she observed as the horse was unloaded under the Duke's watchful eye. With any luck, she wouldn't have to see him before dinner this evening.

Cora managed to keep herself busy and away from the stables the rest of the day. As much as it pained her to stay away, she managed to find time for some walking and reading.

She had chosen an ice-blue satin gown with a darker blue skirt and train for dinner this evening. The gown was subtle compared to some of her other evening gowns. Nodding to her maid, she stood from her dressing table, and after one last look in the mirror, she left the safety of her bedchamber.

To her surprise, she found not only her father and Hightower in the drawing room, but her brother and his two friends. Refusing to give Augustus the satisfaction, she graciously acknowledged both young men as her brother introduced them. The Earl of Falkirk and Viscount Winchester. Both blond, tall, and otherwise most unremarkable in her eyes.

She turned her attention to their guest, Hightower. He stood near the hearth with her father. "Your Grace,

I apologize I wasn't available when you arrived. I trust your stallion had a safe journey?"

"He did. Thank you for asking. I was just telling your father what an efficient and well-run stable he has," he replied with a subtle smirk.

"It is," she acknowledged. "But it is a training stable. It's important everyone works together and on a schedule. I believe that's been achieved."

Her father interrupted to keep the subject on track without Cora giving herself away. "I explained to the Duke how G.S. has gone to personally deliver the mare back to her owner in York."

She nodded. "Yes, he's very hands-on with not only the horses, but the owners. He personally oversees every detail of the training and passes it on to the owner."

"I look forward to meeting him once he's finished with Apollo."

"I believe you'll be most impressed," she replied. Cora shifted her gaze to her brother, who was talking with his two friends, but watching her at the same time. When their eyes met, he smiled mischievously, like he had when he was a young boy. Quickly she shifted her focus back to Hightower.

She quietly noted the huge difference between the Duke and her brother and his friends. They were jovial and still acted like young colts who hadn't yet accepted their place in life, though Augustus was trying his best to act as though he were ready to take his duties seriously. That is, until his two friends arrived. Now he was showing off with his friends, boasting about their conquests, when they thought they were alone and making comparisons between themselves. Instead of the caring brother she'd known, he returned loud and boastful and overly opinionated about everything.

Hightower, however, took his position seriously. She wondered if he'd really ever been the rogue she'd heard him rumored to be. He had never really displayed that side to her. On one occasion he mentioned something about having three sisters who needed his attention. Inheriting a title often forced young men to grow up in a hurry. Certainly they were groomed for their future positions. Augustus had been, though he had been a most difficult pupil. She quietly wondered what the Duke might have been like as a child.

For this evening, however, she needed to keep her wits about her. She couldn't trust Augustus since it was obvious he and his friends had been drinking prior to coming to dinner. Her father kept an eye on them but wouldn't say a word unless they said or did something out of sorts.

Fortunately for everyone, the dinner gong sounded, announcing dinner was served. She accompanied her father into the dining room, followed by Hightower, and then her brother and his friends. Her father had never been one on formality when it came to small gatherings such as this, and seated her next to Hightower, with Viscount Winchester on her other side. She held her breath as Augustus and his friend Falkirk sat across from them.

Her father and Hightower were having a conversation on estate management, keeping her from having to make small talk with him. The older man seemed to genuinely care for Hightower, and she was glad he had someone he could converse with, because he certainly wasn't going to get it with her brother. At least not right now.

Winchester, glass of wine in hand, began to speak

with her as though she were one of the hot house flowers of the *ton*. His conversation and questions, if that's indeed what they were, were shallow and predictable. Asking her about what she liked to read or if she really enjoyed being stuck up in the wilds of Scotland. Cora tried to be cordial as best she could. She hated when men looked down on her and treated her as though she had no real thoughts of her own.

She was grateful when the soup was served. Cook had prepared her mouthwatering creamy asparagus, a favorite, with its light and delicate flavor. Surely that would keep Winchester busy for a while, but he was too busy to notice her anyway, having his crystal wine glass refilled.

Cora turned to Hightower. "I trust you had an uneventful journey, Your Grace?"

"I did. Railroads make travel so much more appealing than a carriage, don't you agree?"

"Absolutely. I don't think I could make the journey between London and here without the rail," she replied. She glanced over at Augustus and kept her eyes on him. He was speaking with Falkirk but kept glancing at her. What was he up to?

The rest of the soup course was without any major conversation, much to Cora's relief. When the poached salmon with crème sauce was served, it was quite noticeable that her brother and his friends were well into their cups, and their father didn't approve.

"I understand you've brought Cora your racer to work out some problems he's having?"

Hightower nodded, his face unreadable as he set his fork down. "It is correct. I've brought him for training under your father's renowned trainer. He has a couple of issues, and I thought it was best if someone else sorted him out. I'm too close to the animal."

Cora held her breath, keeping her eyes focused on her fish. She was afraid if she looked at her brother, he might be more inclined to spout secrets. And she surely didn't want to gaze at Hightower. He might look to her for answers—answers she didn't want to have to give.

"Whatever is bothering him, he'll be right as rain when he's returned to your estate, Your Grace," her father said. "Probably better than he was when you brought him."

"I'm looking forward to just that," Hightower replied. "I have the highest confidence in your trainer."

"Augustus says you ride astride. Why would a lady of good breeding want to do that? It's quite unheard of," Winchester asked with disapproval in his voice, as he picked up his fork.

"Sidesaddles are unsafe. Unlike most young ladies, I love horses and love the thrill of riding in other places besides the park or a safe trail," she replied. "And I can assure you I'm not the only young lady of good breeding who rides this way."

"No wife of mine will ride astride. It's an embarrassment. I'm surprised your father allows it."

Cora put down her fork and went for her goblet of wine. "Then I pity whoever it is who is unfortunate enough to become your wife. With regards to my father, he's always been more forward-thinking than some of you younger gentlemen."

Winchester arched a brow. "Most young ladies marry whom they are told to." He stifled a grin.

She took a sip of wine and set her glass back on the table and gazed at her dinner partner. "As I said, thankfully my father is more forward-thinking in these matters."

Cora turned to Hightower in order to let Winchester stew on their conversation. Miserable prig!

"I understand you're quite good with a bow, Your Grace."

Sebastian arched a brow as he gave her a lop-sided grin. "I do enjoy both hunting and target with a bow. Have you ever used one?"

"Many times, Your Grace. I'm fairly well learned in a crossbow as well."

"Really? Those can be difficult even for me."

"Perhaps we can have a match while you're here."

He smiled warmly. "I look forward to it."

Augustus, however, couldn't keep quiet. Too much drink made him loose-tongued, and not always in a good way.

"You should rise early one morning while you are here, Your Grace, and watch my sister gallop horses on the track. It's a sight to behold. I can't say there's another woman who trains racers the way she does," Augustus said smugly. He sat back, crystal goblet in hand while a footman removed his plate.

Cora held her breath and stared vehemently at her brother. Not daring to look at Hightower, she glanced to her father, who had obviously heard Augustus's declaration.

"Yes, it is," the Duke replied. "Lady Cora on occasion has been known to assist in the horses' training."

Hightower nodded and gazed at Cora. "I would love to see that sometime. I know you are a remarkable rider, Lady Cora."

"Thank you, Your Grace."

"Come on, Cor, tell His Grace everything. I imagine he'd love to know he's leaving his beloved stallion to train with a *woman*." He stared at Hightower. "There is no one else, Your Grace. My sister is the sole trainer. Her story was all a lie."

"Enough, Augustus!" her father boomed.

"I'm sorry, Papa. I only thought Hightower should know, since it is our desire to find Cora a husband, and she won't have time for being foolish with horses once she weds."

Cora continued to stare at her brother in disbelief. She couldn't believe that he would betray a family confidence like that. It left her speechless.

"Is this true, Lady Cora?" she heard Winchester ask.

She nodded her head but ignored Winchester. Instead, she turned her attention to Hightower.

"It is true, Your Grace. I've been training racers for years, but with my father's blessing have kept my identity a secret because no man would entrust his animal to a woman. It's just not done."

"So you lie to everyone," Hightower murmured.

"Would you have sent Apollo if you'd know I was the one training him? No, I seriously doubt you would."

He gazed hard at her with an arched brow. "This is not the first time you've deceived me, Lady Cora. I shall have to reconsider what I'm going to do."

Cora nodded, her head held high. "I understand, Your Grace." She pushed her chair back, a footman helping her as she rose. "If you gentlemen will excuse me, I seem to have lost my appetite."

She fled the dining room and bolted up the stairs. It wasn't like her to run away from anything. This was different. Hightower was a guest, and no, she hadn't been truthful with him, and now her brother had gone and purposely ruined everything. Why couldn't he have just stayed away on the Continent? Everything had been running smoothly while he'd been away at school and abroad. Damn him!

She felt angry, embarrassed, and incredibly sad all at the same time. If Hightower took his stallion and left, there was no stopping him from telling everyone that the Duke of Dover's daughter was his prized trainer. Not only would her father be scrutinized for letting a woman, his daughter no less, train winning Thoroughbreds, he might also be laughed at and seen as an indulgent old man.

Cora, on the other hand, would be whispered about, and would never be invited anywhere by anyone in society. Not that she cared. She might be ruined in the eyes of society, but none of that mattered. She only cared because of her father. She had never set out to cause him any embarrassment. Perhaps it was time she considered purchasing her own farm and moving her training operation.

Her immediate concern was Hightower and how to keep him from bolting, taking with him Apollo's Gold. She deceived him once before when she convinced her father to purchase the horses from Tattersall's from under him. Would he be as forgiving this time?

The Duke didn't seem the sort who was hard and cold but being duped and embarrassed in front of peers might change his mind this time. The best thing she could do was stay out of his way. Tomorrow would be another day, and she prayed he would be in a forgiving mood.

Finding herself restless, unable to sit in the small room, Cora made her way down the back stairs to the kitchen. There she slipped past the staff, out the back door and towards the gardens. Perhaps a walk among the roses would help her, as she found her anger toward her brother raging.

~

"I DON'T KNOW why she's so upset," he heard the Duke's son Augustus say. "The truth was bound to come out. I simply thought Hightower should be made aware of what he's committed to."

"It wasn't up to you to tell!" Dover spat.

"Oh, but it was, Papa. She needs to quit this foolishness and accept the life she's been handed. She's a woman, and therefore needs to marry and produce heirs for her husband. That's her place. Not training powerful stallions."

The older man rose from his chair, ignoring his son. "Hightower, would you care to join me in my study for some brandy?"

Sebastian nodded. "Of course, Your Grace."

He followed the Duke out of the dining room, down the hall to his study. The Duke closed the door after they entered and motioned for Sebastian to sit in one of the leather chairs in front of the fire. While he did, Dover walked over to the nearby sideboard and poured two generous servings of brandy. He passed one to Hightower as he sat next to him.

"I must apologize for both my children's behavior."

"No, you don't. They're grown and have their own opinions and ways of doing things... though I am a bit surprised you would go along with Lady Cora's deception."

The Duke swirled the amber liquid, staring deeply as he did. "Let me ask you a question—would you have sent your stallion here if you'd known a woman would be training him? I doubt it."

"I have no idea—probably not."

"She's got away with the horses, and she's proven herself time and time again. Any horses I have put into her hands have come up winners. The ones I've sent elsewhere for training have not fared as well."

"I see. Though it was still a shock when Augustus revealed her secret." Sebastian took a long drink and set the snifter on a table.

"I apologize for my son. He seems to be determined to see his sister married off, even if it means divulging her secrets. He and his friends..."

"You needn't apologize for him. He's a grown man."

Dover nodded "True. One day he will be duke, and I've raised him as one would his heir. I tried to instill values on both him and his sister."

"He's merely going through what a lot of men his age do. Give him some time—I'm sure he'll turn around."

"I suppose, though he seems to have his mind set on ruining his sister's life. At least the part she loves."

"He just wants her to find a good marriage," Sebastian replied. "Even if his methods are somewhat unconventional."

"Augustus has always been jealous of his sister. Why, and what caused him to be, I can't say."

"Hopefully, he'll realize he's wronged her," Sebastian said.

"He'll never admit it. Augustus has an old-fashioned idea when it comes to women and marriage. Whomever he ends up marrying, it will not be for love, I'm afraid."

"And your daughter won't marry unless it's for love," Sebastian replied.

"No, she won't, and that's part of her and her

brother's differences. He wants her to marry for money and power."

"To be seen and not heard, which with Lady Cora is impossible."

The two men shared a laugh, the older man nodding. "My daughter is not the sort to be a submissive, obedient wife."

Sebastian understood. Lady Cora would prove to be a most lively sort of wife, and there was nothing wrong with that. "I would have to agree with you. She would prove to be a challenge to any man."

Dover stared into the fire, nodding. "If you don't mind me asking, what of you? Are you waiting to marry for love?"

Sebastian sighed. "I've never given it much thought. I always thought when the right woman came along, I would know it. So yes, I suppose I'm waiting to marry for love."

"Don't wait too long. The longer you do, the narrower the playing field becomes."

Sebastian grinned. "Or I can resort to one of the many young debutantes that makes her debut each season."

Dover barked out a laugh. "Or perhaps one who's on her second or third season."

"The idea of endless balls and facing all those mothers parading their young daughters in front of me makes my stomach lurch."

"I remember."

The pair sat in a comfortable silence for a few minutes while each finished their brandy. Sebastian felt at ease with the older man, which was a rare thing, given the circumstances. He would have thought the Duke would have used the time to convince him that his daughter would be a perfect choice for a wife. But he didn't.

"If you'll excuse me, Your Grace, I think I'd like to get some fresh air before I retire," Sebastian announced, noting the hour grew late.

"The gardens are especially beautiful on a moonlit night."

Sebastian nodded. "I'll have my answer regarding my stallion in the morning," Sebastian replied. He rose from his chair and headed for the door.

A few minutes later Sebastian stepped into the gardens. The Duke had been right. The moon was full, giving plenty of light to the pathways. He needed to clear his head after what he'd learned at dinner. What should he do with Apollo? Should he trust him to Lady Cora, even though she and her father had been less than honest and forthcoming with him?

He recalled his conversation with Lady Cora's father earlier. Dover believed in her abilities, but then, he was her father. The Duke had made some valid points. All his own horses had thrived under her hand, and horses sent here had been turned around.

Perhaps what he needed to do is observe her for a day or so. Watch her work, see how she interacted and handled her charges. Even allow her to ride Apollo. That would be the thing to do. If his stallion responded to her in a positive way, it might be for the best to leave him under her care. Apollo was a smart animal, not one to be fooled by anyone. If he didn't like a person, he let them know. Otherwise, he was good-natured and willing to do whatever was asked of him.

Sebastian continued to walk down the path, hands behind his back and deep in thought. Turning a corner, he came upon a bench, occupied by none other than Lady Cora. He had to smile at the sight of her and continued toward her, realizing his feelings about her were starting to shift. He actually enjoyed her conversation and wit and looked forward to it when she wasn't around.

"Lady Cora, I see we both are taking advantage of this lovely evening," he said.

She looked up at him and blinked as though he'd surprised her. "You have to take advantage of every good day or evening here, Your Grace. You never know, it might rain yet again tomorrow."

"I believe you're right," he replied, and gestured toward the bench. "Do you mind? Please, have a seat."

He wasn't sure which way to direct the conversation, so decided better to be safe. "I take it this is a favorite spot of yours."

She nodded. "Yes, it is a place I like to come to reflect."

"When you don't wish to be found?"

She smiled wickedly. "No, I have another spot for that."

He arched a brow. "Intriguing, and mysterious."

"You think so?"

"Yes. Even I have a private place on my estate I go to when I wish to be alone."

"Away from your duties as duke?"

"Yes," he murmured. He felt his body awakening in ways he wasn't sure it should be. Yes, she was quite attractive, and he'd had more than his fair share of daydreams about her.

"I have to apologize for misleading you, Your Grace."

"About what?" he asked innocently.

"The situation about my training horses. If men knew the trainer they were sending their animals to was a woman, they wouldn't. Something I need to work on."

"I will admit it shocked me for a moment, but upon thinking it through, I can say I'm not really surprised."

She smiled. "I so love that you disapprove, Your Grace."

"Sebastian, please. 'Your Grace makes me feel like an old man, and I never said I disapproved. I was merely surprised when your brother told me."

"So, you've reached a decision?"

He shook his head. "No." The look of disappointment on her face suddenly was something he couldn't stand to see. "I thought to see how you and Apollo get along. I'd like to watch you ride him before I make any decisions."

"My father convinced you of this?"

"No. I don't feel it would be fair to judge you solely because of your sex. It's obvious you have a vast knowledge of horses, as you proved at Tattersall's."

"You won't be sorry, Your Grace... Sebastian," she replied. "And thank you."

He grinned at her boldness. "I haven't agreed to anything yet, Lady Cora. I merely want to see you in action."

"As you wish."

He sighed and gazed at her. "The world is changing for women, as I'm sure you're aware. Is it going to change you?"

"No, not at all. Women are being allowed more freedoms, and fortunately for me, my father's agreeable to it. I have my own money from training, and don't have to rely on an allowance from my father." She smiled warmly at the thought. "He still gives me one, even though I protest."

"What else?"

"The training here is my business. My father merely attaches his name to it, since as we discussed, men would be hesitant to send their horses to a woman. One day I'll have my own property to build my own stables."

"Why not stay here?"

"When the time comes and Augustus is duke, I won't abide by my brother's rules."

"Hopefully that won't happen for many years," he said.

"Yes," she said.

"Would you care to join me on an early morning ride? I find it the perfect time to prepare myself for the day ahead."

"I would love to, but would you ride Apollo?" she inquired.

"No," he said, shaking his head of black curls. "Your stablemaster mentioned there was a gelding at my disposal while I'm here, should I care to ride."

He rose, not trusting himself if he sat this close to her. A part of him wanted to give in to his impulses and take her in his arms and kiss her hard. The other part wanted to keep a distance.

She stood and gazed at him. "Would you like to walk a while? I would enjoy the company."

"I'd be delighted." What made him say that? He couldn't afford to let his feelings get in the way. Not if he was to make a rational decision regarding Apollo.

He offered his arm, and they began to walk further down the path. Finally, they came upon a fountain.

"This was a favorite place my mother would come when she wanted quiet. We always knew where she was, but we left her alone."

He nodded. "I can see why she liked it so much. Do you miss her?"

"Sometimes. It hasn't been easy, but my father's done a good job raising me. I'm not the most cooperative student. I hate being stuck inside with tutors. What did I need with French when I could be outside with my horses?"

"Do you ever feel isolated out here?"

"No, never. Besides, I accompany my father to London or Edinburgh quite often. Mostly when I'm between clients. After a week, I'm ready to return."

He barked out a laugh. "I'm the same, though my duties keep me there, far longer than I'd like. I'm always ready to retire to my estate as soon as I can."

She flashed a dazzling smile at him. He couldn't resist any longer. He tipped up her chin, and his mouth came down hard on hers. Her lips instinctively opened to him as his tongue met hers, as they discovered each other. This was no gentle kiss. He was kissing her in a blaze of passion. He shifted closer and spread his fingers on her lower back. Confused by his actions, he ended the kiss.

She made a sound, an urgent plea for more. Their eyes met before his mouth crashed down on hers once again. This time she opened eagerly to him, her arms going around his neck.

Dear God, if he kept on, he'd be seducing her and having his way with her right here in the garden. He stared down at her longingly. She was exquisite.

"I apologize."

She grinned. "Please, don't apologize. I'll have you know I'm rarely chaperoned here. In London perhaps, but not here."

"Perhaps your father should reconsider."

"Why? Are you afraid of your own feelings, Sebastian?"

"No. I've never met a woman quite like you, Cora."

"Then why should we deny our feelings or desires?"

"Because you're a lady and an innocent," he replied.

"I knew the moment I met you, you were a gentleman. No one else would have stood for what I did at Tattersall's."

"What you did at Tattersall's was inexcusable. The only reason you got away with it is because of who your father is. Quite frankly, I was surprised by his lack of reaction."

She smiled. "That's because my father knows I have a superior knowledge to most men when it comes to horses."

"If you'd been my daughter, you would have gotten a good thrashing and talking-to when we returned home."

"How do you know I didn't?"

He arched a dark brow. "Because your father indulges you."

"Yes, he does. As I said, Your Grace, you were a gentleman about the incident. I appreciate that."

A gentleman? Partially, perhaps. There had been a time in the not-so-distant past where he'd been anything but. With Cora, he found himself acting differently. Cora was a strong, independent young woman, something he found refreshing. He could speak to her about anything, far more than most women, and unlike other women, she was comfortable with who she was. She was the first woman in a number of years who made all those feelings of protection, want, and desire resurface. This time it wasn't all about bedding a woman, it was the two of them getting to know the other. Was he mad?

"I try," he replied.

She looked up at the sky, taking his arm once again. "It is getting late. I suppose we should go in. I thought rather than an early morning ride, we could do a picnic tomorrow."

"I thought you had horses to train."

"I do. I intend to give Apollo a go on my track, re-member? I'm usually at the barn no later than seven," she replied. "And that's before breakfast."

"Then I'll see you at the barn first light."

She looked up at him, the edges of her mouth curled up. "You don't mind my change of plans?"

"Not at all. I'm quite interested in seeing how you and Apollo rub along. A picnic will be a nice change. I can't remember the last time I went on one."

They entered the drawing room. The house was quiet except for the tick of a clock. He found himself looking forward to spending more time with Cora.

12

After a night of fitful rest, Cora dressed at dawn's light to begin her day. She would meet Sebastian at the stables and he would watch her ride Apollo. He would see she was a competent trainer, as good or better than any man. Satisfied, Sebastian would leave the stallion in her care.

She found him stroking the velvety nose of his stallion, talking lowly to him as a young groom brushed him. If he noticed her arrival, he did not let on.

"Good morning, Your Grace."

He gazed at her, a lopsided grin on his handsome face. "Good morning, Lady Cora. Are you ready to put Apollo through his paces?

"Yes, I'm looking forward to it."

She stood to one side as the groom saddled the stallion, trying her best not to look at Sebastian. "You said you stopped racing him. What have you been doing with him?"

She knew the answer, she just wanted to hear it from his lips. Those wonderful, kissable lips.

"I put him in a small pasture alone during the day. Let him have some time off."

Cora nodded. "Do you think it helped?"

"Yes, I believe it did. He seems calmer."

"Sometimes, giving them time off is all it takes," she replied. "Why don't we see how he responds."

They followed the young groom out of the stables to the training track, where Cora stood on a mounting block and threw her leg over the stallions back. He stood calm as she made adjustments to the saddle before gathering the reins and walking him onto the track. She stroked his neck, patted it, all while talking to him.

She started him off in a trot to learn his gaits and warm him up. Cora could tell the stallion had been well trained. Most youngsters would want to immediately break into a gallop, Apollo listened to her, waiting for her commands. Sebastian had done well making sure the animal had manners. Many who'd come to her did not, which made her job harder.

After two laps around the course, she decided to open him up. She urged the youngster into a slow gallop. He immediately obeyed, not fighting for his head, wanting to charge forward. Once again she was impressed with the training the stallion had already received. He was a delight to ride.

Deciding he was warmed up enough, she leaned over and whispered to him, as she loosened the reins and gave him his head. All she did to open him up was cluck to him and add pressure with her legs. The stallion did the rest. He ran like the wind, giving her everything he had. Her job would be easy. There wouldn't be a lot she would have to do. Obviously he'd soured on whoever had been riding him, and Sebastian had yet to find a suitable replacement. She would help him find the perfect rider.

She reined the stallion in and slowed him down.

He was every bit as good as Sebastian had said he was. He just needed some direction, and of course, the right person to ride him.

Cora let the reins drop, patting his neck for a job well done as she walked back to the entrance where Sebastian and the groom stood. Apollo was still breathing hard, even though she'd walked him around the track one lap. She slid down off his back with ease. She then instructed the young man to walk the stallion to cool him down before bathing him and then feeding him a much-deserved meal.

"What did you think?" Sebastian asked eagerly.

"He's magnificent. You've trained him well."

"But..."

She grinned. "I think all he needs is the right person to ride him when he's racing. It's obvious to me he's soured on whoever you had riding him before, and you just haven't found the right person."

"That's all?"

"I don't think he needs a lot in regard to training. You've trained him well. He's well behaved and listens," she replied.

"How long?"

"How long what, Your Grace?"

"Sebastian," he growled lowly. "How much time do you think you need with him, and how do I go about finding a decent rider?"

"We're not alone," she whispered. The groom was well ahead of them and probably couldn't hear them. There was something delightful about sparring with him.

"So? Is he your chaperone as well?"

"No, and I have no need of one. I am perfectly capable of taking care of myself."

He grinned "I never said you weren't."

"You're getting off track, Your Grace. We were talking about Apollo, nothing else."

"Whatever you say."

"Stop it!"

"Stop what? I'm trying to have a conversation with you."

She rolled her eyes. "Yes, about chaperones and whether I need one. Which by the way is none of your business."

"What else would you like to talk about? What a pleasant day it is?"

"You are so exasperating!" she said.

A deep laugh came from deep inside him. "Good! I'm glad we agree on something."

"Sebastian, stop. Now."

He nodded with a devilish grin. "How long do you think you will need with Apollo? Can you help find a new rider?"

"No more than a month. I will help you find a rider, don't worry."

"Very well."

She gazed up at him as they walked. "As a matter of fact, there is a race at Musselburgh in six weeks I think would be perfect for him. Why don't I ready him for it? I'll see if one of my riders might be available."

"Do you think he'll be ready?"

"He could go today, but I would like a chance to get to know him better before I bring in one of my riders."

The Duke gazed ahead at his prized stallion before answering. "You really think he'll be ready?"

"I do," she replied.

"Very well. I'll leave him with you. The two of you are obviously forming a bond, and if you think you can improve him, then you have my support."

"Thank you, Sebastian. You won't be sorry."

"I know I won't. I only worry your brother may be a bother. He seemed so set in ruining your set-up here last night. I'd hate for Apollo to be part of it."

She snorted. "Augustus will do no such thing. Papa won't allow it. He's not duke yet, and he has his own estate to look after. Besides he was far into his cups last night."

"Very well. We have a deal," he replied.

She hesitated. There were two more horses requiring her attention this morning. Before she knew it, it would be time to ready herself for their picnic, and she certainly didn't want to join Sebastian smelling like a horse. A strange idea, as it usually never bothered her, nor did she care. For some strange reason she was willing to bathe and change out of her breeches for a dress.

"My father can finalize the cost with you. I leave that in his expert hands," she said. "If we're to go on our picnic, I fear I must get back to work. I'll meet you in the grand hall in say, two hours?" Two hours was pushing it, but neither of the other horses needed much extra work, and she could have her groom warm them up before she rode.

"I'll go in search of your father, and I'll meet up with you in two hours," he replied. "Thank you, Lady Cora. You've lifted a heavy weight off my shoulders. I'm glad Apollo's still got a chance at racing."

"Don't thank me, Your Grace. Thank Apollo. All I did was listen to him. Horses are a lot smarter than people give them credit for."

With that he bowed and turned, leaving her to go in search of her next project. A gelding who had a vile temper from being mishandled by his last trainer. Unlike Apollo, he was going to take some time. A lot of time.

• • •

SHE MET him in the grand hallway. He turned as he heard her approach, nodding in her direction.

"The cart is waiting, and our basket is in the back," he said with a grin.

"I have the perfect place in mind. You'll love it."

They neared the cart, pulled by a sturdy bay gelding. "Would you like to drive?" he asked.

"No, go ahead. I'll guide you. It's not all that far, but the view is worth it."

He helped her into the cart, walked around to the other side, and climbed in beside her. Gathering the reins he urged the gelding forward. She pointed him in the direction of a small path leading away from the manor. The narrow path wound up a steep hill, which she knew all too well. It was one of her most favorite places to go to, especially when she'd been a young girl and wanted to get away from Augustus and his constant teasing.

"Where are we going?" he asked, without taking his eyes off the path.

"You'll see. All I'll tell you is it's a favorite spot of mine. You can see for miles."

They carried on in a comfortable silence. Cora observed the Duke out of the corner of her eye. He was wearing fawn breeches. His legs were well muscled and filled out the breeches quite nicely. He wore a shiny pair of brown leather knee-high boots meant for riding. The coat he wore was well tailored and gave her a sense of how much time he spent doing activities other than drinking and writing. It was evident, by his well-toned physique, he loved the outdoors.

"Here, go to the right. We can leave the cart by that

boulder and walk the rest of the way. It isn't far, I promise," she said.

He nodded and did as she had instructed. As much as it pained her to wait, she did, letting him help her down.

"I'll take care of the horse if you can manage the basket," he said as he removed his hands from her waist. Had he felt the spark? Or had it been her imagination?

"Very well," she replied. "I'll be right over there in the clearing under that large oak tree."

He nodded and handed her the basket.

She took the basket from him, another jolt soaring through her as their fingers touched. She walked off and headed toward the tree, which overlooked miles of breathtaking countryside.

Cora unlatched the top of the basket and found the tartan cotton cloth. It billowed in the breeze as she shook it out. Once it landed, she pinned down the edges with rocks.

He joined her as she began setting out the food. He sat down against the tree and watched her, then the landscape before him.

"It's beautiful here. I can see why this is your favorite place."

"Isn't it?" She unwrapped a plate of meat pasties Cook had sent along with them. "Cook makes some excellent meat pies. Would you like one?"

He nodded. "I would, and while you're tending to that, I'll pour us some wine."

The pies were beautifully brown and still warm. She held one up. "How many?"

"Two, and your cook is to be commended. A smart idea for a picnic. No fuss of knives and forks."

She placed his pies on a plate and handed them to

him. "There is some cheese, as well as apples, and I believe some of her delicious tarts."

Accepting a glass of wine, she leaned back to enjoy her meal.

"Do you do this often?"

"What? Come here with a picnic? I did when I was a girl, but I rarely have time for such luxuries these days."

"You should try harder," he drawled, as he popped the last of his meat pie in his mouth.

She couldn't help but smile. "What about you? Do you have time for picnics, or do your ducal duties keep you from such pleasures?"

"Sadly, the latter is true."

"Then you must try to go on one next time you're at your estate."

Cora watched as he finished his glass of wine, saying nothing. She wanted him to carry the conversation. Certainly he'd heard enough of her go on and on about horses.

"Tell me, have you brought other men here? For a picnic?"

She snorted quite unladylike as she faced him. "No, you're the first, if you don't count Augustus. He's been here a few times with me when we were growing up."

"I apologize. That is none of my business."

"No need. I could never bring any potential suitor here because they would take it... you know what I mean."

"They'd take it as an invitation for something more intimate, more enticing?" he inquired finishing her thoughts.

How did he know her so well?

"Yes, exactly," she replied. She reached for a piece

of cheese he offered her and watched him sitting across from her on the picnic cloth eating a slice of apple. She swallowed hard just looking at him. There was something so erotic about how he sliced the apple and popped it into his mouth.

A wayward lock of black hair kept falling over his face. She noted how thick and black his lashes were. He was something to behold, like a fine painting perhaps. He must have felt her gazing upon him as he glanced up and locked eyes with her. Neither spoke but there was some sort of spark in the air that hadn't been there a few minutes ago.

He sat up, moving his plate to one side.

She made some sort of noise in the back of her throat as she found herself in his arms. His body was warm and hard as his mouth captured hers, telling her to open her mouth to his. Cora wound her arms around his neck and let his velvety tongue tangle with hers. She found her attention consumed by him, as though they had never left off from the night before. She moaned under his passionate, all-consuming kisses.

As the kiss finally ended, she moved her mouth just enough to nip his lower lip. One of his hands slid around and cupped her bottom, her dress splayed up above her knees. "Woman, you are going to be the death of me," he rasped. He shifted his position just enough that she was sure to feel his hardened cock against her thigh.

This time he nipped her lower lip and stared down into her eyes.

"Sebastian," she whispered.

"What?" he groaned, as his mouth came down on hers again, this time more urgent than the last.

She wanted him to ruin her more than anything

else she'd ever wanted. Did this mean she was falling in love with him, or was it merely desire? She was certain he felt the same way, but perhaps he had not figured that out yet? The one thing she vowed would never happen was becoming reality.

"More..." she whispered once again, with more urgency.

His weight lifted as he groaned. "Come, time to go. Before we do something we might both regret."

"I highly doubt that."

He sat up, adjusting his clothing and look out over the land below them. She watched him through hooded eyes, admiring his well-muscled physique.

"We've been gone long enough. We need to head back," he said.

She smoothed her dress and batted her eyes at him. "I don't see the urgency, but if you insist." She began to put the plates and other items back in the basket. When she was through, he took the basket and moved it to one side and helped her with the cloth they had been sitting on. For the first time she didn't want this moment to end.

SHE WAS TEMPTING—TOO tempting. Today, however, all the façade melted away. All the pretense and sniping disappeared, and with it he was shown Cora, the real Lady Cora. A delightful, caring, sensual young woman. A woman with passion, who knew exactly what she wanted out of life. Cora would never settle. She would go kicking and screaming if her life was anything other than what she wanted.

He led her back to the cart, holding her hand in one of his, the basket in the other. The path narrowed and he had to let go of her, so he let her lead the way back to the cart. He could watch her from behind, and she would have no idea what being this close to her did to him.

Placing the basket in the back of the cart, he walked around to the front to the horse and readied him for the journey back. Cora was out of sight, but he could hear her rustling around in the basket.

As he turned, she surprised him with two fried fruit pies, one in each hand. "I almost forgot these. Cook made some apple pies, and I'll never hear the end of it if we don't eat at least one."

He accepted the golden-brown pie. "We mustn't disappoint your cook. Thank you."

It was delicious, as everything had been. This, however, was cooked to perfection, with just the right combination of spices and sugar.

He handed her into the cart, then joined her. He clucked the gelding forward, and they rode in silence for a few minutes. Suddenly she snaked her arm through his. "I've enjoyed this very much, Sebastian."

"As have I," he replied. She had no idea how much he had liked their excursion. "What are your plans for the remainder of the afternoon?"

"I'm to meet with the housekeeper, our monthly meeting to go over the household. I avoid it like the plague. She's a perfectly capable woman and doesn't need my interference, but Papa insists," she said. "And you?"

"I thought I'd seek out your father to let him know of my decision."

"What decision is that, Your Grace?" she asked mockingly.

"That I intend to leave Apollo in your care until the race in six weeks."

She brushed a stray lock of hair off her face. "You aren't going to rush back to London, are you?"

"Why? Will you miss me?" He teased with a smile.

"Of course not. I'm far too busy," she replied.

"Then it will please you to know I haven't made firm plans. I thought I might stay a few days and watch you with Apollo, and also to see who you come up with as a rider."

She rolled her eyes. "Finding a rider will take time, Your Grace, but please do feel free to observe."

"I also thought I'd like to take some rides about the countryside. It's so beautiful here."

"I can arrange a more suitable horse for you," she replied.

"Thank you."

He stopped as she turned to face him more squarely.

"Would you care to take a turn in the gardens after tea? You really must see it in the light of day. Especially now when everything is blooming."

"I would love to, but I don't know if that is such a good idea unless your maid comes along to chaperone."

She grinned. "Sebastian? You're worried about my virtue after our picnic? I can take care of myself and hardly need a chaperone. Especially in broad daylight and in the gardens. I'm hardly some young, doe-eyed girl."

"I never said you were," he replied.

"Then you'll join me? On the terrace at four?"

He nodded. "I look forward to it, Lady Cora."

Once they arrived at the manor, he helped her down. She headed inside, leaving him to fend for himself. She didn't look forward to household meetings.

She stopped and turned around. "I'll see you at four, Your Grace."

He nodded and held up the basket. "I'll return this to the kitchens and see if I can't snag another pie."

She giggled and was gone. Just like that, leaving him with his cock all in a muddle. His breeches bulged from what she'd done to him, leaving him to carry the basket directly in front of him.

Leaving the kitchens with another pie in hand, Sebastian found the Duke in his study. He entered, finding the older man sitting behind his desk. He looked up from a pile of papers.

"Hightower, come, sit. I take it you've had a productive day so far?"

"I have Your Grace," he replied, as he sat in one of the two leather chairs in front of the Duke's desk.

"Did you see my daughter ride your stallion?"

"I did, and I was as impressed as I had no doubt I would be," he replied. "Which brings me to part of the reason I'm here."

"Go on."

"I've decided, after watching her with Apollo to leave him in her training for the next six weeks. There is a race then, and she thinks it would benefit him."

"Excellent," the older man replied.

"I'll have my man of business send you the funds," he drawled. "Lady Cora said to discuss that with you as she detests bookkeeping."

He smiled. "Aye, she does. Just like she dislikes meeting with the housekeeper."

Sebastian sat back in his chair and tried not to smile. "I thought I would stay on for a few days. I'd like to see more of the estate and countryside before I head back to London."

"Stay as long as you wish. You don't spend the summers at your country seat?"

"I do, but I have a few things needing my attention in London before I can do so."

"Lady Cora can of course see you have a suitable horse, and a guide for your excursions. Who knows, I might join you one day."

"I would like that."

"Then it's settled," he replied. "I am expecting my son shortly. He's changed since he left for the continent."

"That sometime happens."

"The man he came back as is far from the young man who left."

"I'm sure he'll settle once his friends leave. He has his own estate to tend to, so that ought to occupy his time."

The Duke nodded. "True, though he seems bent on marrying his sister off."

"I noticed. Any reason why, if I might ask?"

"He thinks I indulge her far too much, which I admit I do. With her married, Augustus believes he and I will have more time."

"I take it he doesn't believe women should stray from being wives and mothers?"

"No, he doesn't. He was in his cups, but he is determined to see her married. He doesn't believe women should be training horses, especially racers."

"He seemed determined to tarnish her reputation," Sebastian said quietly. He would be damned if Cora's brother ruined her reputation, either as a woman or as a trainer.

"He does, which is why I don't trust him, and why he's coming here this afternoon to meet with me. I want to get to the bottom of this before it gets out of hand."

Sebastian rose, standing to his full height. "Then I'll leave you, Your Grace. I look forward to seeing you later."

"Can I offer you a whiskey before you go?"

"No, I have my own correspondence to tend to and need to have a clear head when I write my man of business," he replied with a grin. "Another time."

"Of course, and if I can be of any help while you're here, please feel free to find me."

"Thank you, Your Grace."

Sebastian left the Duke's study feeling anxious. Why, he had no idea, but knowing Cora's brother was expected by the Duke this afternoon didn't set well with him. The man seemed to have turned into a scoundrel, bent on destruction if he did not get his way.

Instead of lingering on matters that really weren't his business, he made his way upstairs to his rooms. He had letters to write, even if he had a niggling Augustus was not as he appeared. Hopefully he would leave his friends at his estate and come alone. Perhaps he was a completely different person without their influence.

He sat down at the writing desk and took out a sheet of paper, but not before he poured himself a whiskey from the decanter left in his rooms. He took a swallow and began to write his man, directing him to send funds to the Duke for Apollo's training, with the balance to be paid at the end.

Once he finished, Sebastian prepared the letter to go out, and went in search of a footman who was outside his door. He gave the young man the letter and instructions. Returning to his room he finished his whiskey and sat down in a comfortable chair in front of the windows. The view from his rooms was magnificent. Mountains everywhere, making him wonder what their history was.

Before he realized it, he fell asleep. When he stirred, he wasn't entirely sure how much time had passed, but assumed it was mid-afternoon.

He walked into the dressing room and found his majordomo putting away shirts he'd taken to be pressed. He nodded and walked over to a basin and splashed cold water on his face.

"You should have woken me," he said.

"You were obviously tired, Your Grace."

"I'm to have tea with Lady Cora on the terrace. I suppose I should change boots," he muttered staring down at his dusty boots. "I don't think these will do at all."

"If you'll sit, I'll bring you another pair," the major-domo replied. "May I ask how long we're to stay here, now that you've had a chance to make your decision about Apollo?"

Sebastian nodded. "I thought I'd like to see a bit more of the country around here, so I believe we'll be staying another four days or so. Is that a problem?"

"Not at all, Your Grace. I merely wanted to be prepared for whatever may arise."

"Right now, the only thing is meeting Lady Cora for tea," he replied with a grin.

A few moments later he walked out of his rooms and headed downstairs to the drawing room where she had told him they would be taking tea. As he was walking, it occurred to him just how big the house/castle was. The castle could swallow his country home whole and still have plenty of room to spare. This was Scotland, and much like England, there was an abundance of castles and great estates.

He would have to have Cora give him a tour. Places like this had always fascinated him. The rooms went on and on. Right now, however, his mind was somewhere besides historical aspects of a castle. They were with Lady Cora. He groaned silently as it suddenly occurred to him that this outspoken, independent woman was indeed getting under his skin in a most delightful fashion. He'd had numerous daydreams of bedding her and had no doubt she would not disappoint. Still, he reminded himself, she was an innocent, and didn't need to be scared her first time. Her first time would be with him if he had anything to say about it. Cora had already sent signals confirming she wanted more than a passionate, devouring kiss.

13

As he stepped out onto the terrace, the first thing Sebastian noticed was Cora, and seated across from her was her father. He tried not to show his disappointment as he approached. How could he, when here she was in a dark-blue muslin dress. He wondered if she had any idea of how beautiful and feminine she looked, dressed as though she'd just stepped out of one of London's finest dressmakers.

"Your Grace. I was beginning to wonder if you had gotten lost," her eyes full of mirth. "My brother failed to show up so I asked Papa to join us."

"Lady Cora, Your Grace," he murmured. "Perhaps Augustus merely forgot."

"It wouldn't be the first time," Cora replied as she poured him a cup of tea and placed it in front of him.

"Yes, but he's gotten worse since he left for the Continent. Before, I could excuse his actions as those of a boyish colt. Now he's simply defiant," the older man said.

"His friends are here, Papa. Perhaps he merely forgot the time."

"Perhaps," he replied. He finished his tea and rose.

"Since Augustus has failed to show, I believe I'll go on my afternoon walk. Zig needs his exercise."

"Very well, Papa. Enjoy your walk."

The older man whistled, and a Scottish deerhound came loping out of nowhere. This one reminded him of his own hunting dogs, though the Duke allowed this one more freedom than his own.

The pair sat silent as they watched the man and his best friend disappear from sight.

"I've never seen such a dog. He's magnificent, though he does eat as much as two men."

"If you're worried about him eyeing you for his afternoon snack, don't. Papa sees he's well fed," she teased.

The corners of his mouth tugged up. "Good to know."

"He does love that dog. They're constant companions. Papa and he take long walks together every day unless it's raining, and even that doesn't too often deter Papa."

"A true Scotsman, your father."

She nodded. "He is."

"I've noticed your accent is more English than Scots. Is it on purpose, or the way you were brought up, perhaps?"

She flashed him a gleaming smile. "I find most Englishmen react better if I don't. Be assured though, I can speak Scots as well as any other native."

"I'm sure when you don't want someone like me to know what you're saying?" he teased.

"Perhaps," she replied smugly. "But then I'd never tell."

Then she turned the table on him, focusing their conversation back around to him. She was good at things like this. Very good.

"Do you like to hunt, Your Grace?"

"Sebastian," he growled.

"There are servants around," she whispered. "It's a simple question, Your Grace. Do you like to hunt?"

He arched a brow and observed her closely. What was she up to? "I don't get much of a chance unless I'm at my estate."

"I'll have to have Papa arrange for a day out. You really must try your luck at hunting a stag while you're here."

"You don't have to do that. I'm sure His Grace has more important matters than to take me on a hunt."

"Nonsense. He'll love it. Augustus has never been interested in hunting or fishing. My father has a passion for both," she replied.

"Your father likes to fish?"

"Fly-fish in the river you saw on the way. Part of it runs through the estate."

He gave her a lopsided grin. "I haven't fly-fished since I was a boy, and we came on holiday to Scotland."

Cora cocked her head. "Really? Then you know the basics."

"I'm sure they'd come back to me," he replied nodding.

She picked up her cup and took a sip of tea. "Then it's settled. I'll speak with him about both," she laughed. "We can't have you returning to London without having done one or both. What would your friends think?"

"Indeed," he replied. "Though I'll let you in on a little secret..."

"What's that, Your Grace?"

He bent over toward her, closing the distance between them. "I don't give a damn what my friends think."

She smiled wickedly. "I knew once I stripped away some of that hardened exterior, there would be something about you I'd like."

"I'm happy to please, Lady Cora," he replied mockingly.

A loud, rather obnoxious voice boomed from the doorway. "What do we have here, Sister? Taking tea with a man? Unchaperoned? Tsk, tsk," Augusta said rather loudly.

"Thank you for your sudden interest in my reputation," Cora replied sarcastically.

"I always have been interested in your honor," he replied, slurring his words while plopping down into the chair their father had occupied minutes ago. "And now that I'm back, I intend to make sure your reputation stays as pure as it was the day you were born."

Cora arched a brow. "I've managed quite nicely without you,"

Sebastian held his breath as he watched this unfold, wondering if he would have to intervene, though Cora seemed more than able to hold her own with her sibling.

"And yet, here you are—having tea with a man, unchaperoned."

"The Duke is a guest, Augustus."

"So I've been told," he replied.

"Papa waited as long as he could. You're late, and you know how he feels about that."

"Yes, I'm sure. Where did he go?"

"Out for a walk."

Augustus threw back his head, looking up at the sky. "Of course. With those damn dogs of his. Sometimes I think he prefers the beasts to either of us."

"Don't be silly. You know how he hates being inside all the time."

Augustus snapped his fingers and a footman appeared out of nowhere. "Bring me a whiskey."

"Augustus..." Cora said.

"What? I might as well enjoy myself if I have to wait on him," he replied, and gazed at her, then at Sebastian and back to Cora. "I'm not interrupting anything am I? The two of you weren't planning an intimate stroll in the gardens, were you?"

Cora rose from her chair. "That's enough!"

Augustus ignored her outburst, turning his attention to Sebastian. Before he did, the footman returned and placed a glass of whiskey in front of him. He swallowed its contents in one gulp and set the glass down on the table with a loud thud.

"You must forgive my sister. She likes men to think she's still all innocent and pure, when she's actually a tart and a tease."

Sebastian looked him square in the eye. "You sister is nothing but a fine, well-mannered young woman, and it would do you good to show her some respect."

Augustus barked out a laugh. "Well, well, well... I don't see how it's possible, but it seems you have an admirer, Cora. I mean what man would want a woman who's like you?"

"Like me?" Cora bit out.

"Yes, like you. What man would want a woman who's outspoken and doesn't know her place. Oh, and takes on hobbies that are best left to men." He shook his head of mussed dark hair.

"I would," Sebastian said. The words had escaped his mouth without thinking, and he silently cursed himself for it. He was not about to sit by idly and watch as this sotted young fool of a brother tore her apart in front of him. He had no right.

"What? You, Your Grace?" he said lazily with a smirk. A smirk Sebastian wished he could knock off his face.

"You heard me. I find Lady Cora to be a breath of fresh air, and I have nothing but the highest regard for her."

"Are you proposing marriage, Hightower? Do you wish to court my sister?"

"That is none of you concern, Augustus," Cora said. She shot Sebastian a look he couldn't read. She wasn't angry with him, but he knew she wasn't exactly happy either.

"Ah, but like I told you, it is. If Papa won't marry you off, I'm afraid I will have to intervene."

Cora shook her head and rose. Sebastian stood as well, waiting for her cue.

"If you won't leave, I will. You've been drinking, Augustus, and you disgust me." She turned to Sebastian. "Come, Your Grace. Papa was wanting me to give you a tour of the castle. He mentioned you had an interest in history."

"I do," he replied. He kept his eye on Augustus who seemed to have completely forgotten they were there, as he was demanding another whiskey be brought.

He followed behind her into the drawing room, where she stopped abruptly. She turned to face him. "I apologize for my brother's behavior. He's his own man and I can't make him change his ways."

Sebastian shook his head. "You shouldn't have to, but I admire you for the way you handle him."

She smiled graciously. "Come, we'll start in the portrait gallery."

"Please, lead the way," he replied. He smiled back at her.

This was turning out to be a far more interesting trip than he first imagined it would be. At least with some of the options Cora had laid out, his days weren't going to be boring while he visited, and perhaps he would get lucky with his fly-fishing skills once he polished them up. It had been quite a while since he'd been fishing, even on his own private lake. It was kept stocked, but it seemed he never had time for the simple pleasures.

Cora was determined to keep Sebastian away from her brother. There was no reason for the Duke to be subjected to Augustus when he was drinking, which seemed to be a daily ritual for him now. Had something changed with her brother? Was that why he drank to excess now or was it simply the way he was going to be, now that he was a man?

There was nothing she could do for her brother. He would have to figure it out on his own, and once he was rid of his friends, she hoped he would return to being the young man she had known. She needed to concentrate on her own affairs. Sebastian was spending far too much money for training, and she didn't wish him to leave here with second thoughts. She had enough time with him before he went back to London to get to know him better.

After having spent time with Sebastian, she found she no longer disliked him like she had when first meeting him. He was kind and seemed genuinely interested. His kisses proved that, for she was certain he cared. Could she risk everything for something with him? No. She'd worked too hard to gain her reputation as a trainer. She could stand on her own two feet without him. Still she hoped they would have time to spend together before he left for London. She enjoyed their time together.

They entered the portrait gallery and began walking through it in silence. It was chilly in here any time of the year. The room ran along one of the outside granite walls. Long-dead relatives, most dressed in their tartan, hung from the walls, looking down at those who entered. She stopped in front of one of her grandfathers.

"This is my father's father, the late Duke. I never really knew him, though sometimes my mind flashes with bits and pieces of him and my grandmother."

"I can see the similarities between him and the one over there of your father." He pointed to a recent portrait of her father.

"Yes. Augustus takes more after my mother's side of the family."

He turned toward her. "Yet you seem to be your father's daughter in every way. The similarities are quite strong."

"They are," she replied. She gazed at him, then the gallery. It was fairly stark except for the portraits, some that had hung here undisturbed for generations. "Come, I'll show you the music room and library."

Sebastian was grateful for having this time alone with Cora. She had awakened something long missing in his life. Certainly, he'd had mistresses, and one or two women he'd seriously considered marriage to, but something always held him back.

He'd cracked through Cora's thick wall of armor, and she was letting him in to the real woman, and he found he liked what he was discovering. More than he originally thought possible. He needed to make his intentions known to her before he left.

Her brother was undoubtably a bother. He was attempting to reinsert himself into her life here when he needed to work on his own matters. Marrying off his sister shouldn't be something Augustus need worry himself about. She wasn't on the shelf or anywhere near being considered a spinster. Far from it. Perhaps Cora was right, that he was being influenced by his friends. Perhaps he would grow bored and move on.

She had shown him through most of the downstairs rooms—the library, which was massive, and one he could spend hours in, looking through the endless shelves of books. Then there had been a morning sitting room the family used, which was tastefully done in greens and golds. After that, a music room. The room was far larger than he anticipated, and a piano sat prominently to one end. A harp sat in a corner, and he wondered whether Cora played it.

They had just finished up a lively discussion about composers when she abruptly changed the subject, startling him.

"Would you like me to show you some of the hidden rooms? Castles, as I'm sure you aware, are notorious for hidden passageways and secret rooms."

"Yes, I would. My own home has one passageway off the Duke's chamber. It was originally a way for the Duke to escape unseen."

"Come, not many know it exists and there are few places to enter. I understand it was used as a place to hide women and children if the castle were under siege. There is also a way to escape, which is to this day quite well hidden. My grandfather did have the entrance locked, and it is not accessible except with a key."

"Lead on. I find things like this quite fascinating. Do you go in there often?"

"Not as much as I used to, but I keep a place in case I need to be alone," she replied. "It's my favorite, because my brother doesn't know if it's existence."

"Intriguing," he said.

"Didn't you have places to go to escape from your siblings or to be alone?"

"Yes, but it's not in the house."

"Now you have my interest piqued," she said.

They had been walking all this time, and she finally stopped in what appeared to be a little-used drawing room. "This used to be my mother's favorite room. Once she died, my father found it hard to spend time in it. But lucky for us, this is where one of the entrances to the passage is."

He nodded and watched in fascination as she approached a bookshelf, and after finding a latch, the panel next to it opened into darkness. She lifted a lantern off the floor and lit it, beckoning him to follow. Once they were both inside, she reversed the process and the door shut. By the lantern he was able to see the narrow passage in front of them and wondered how many people had used this particular passageway in years long gone by.

The passage was dark and musty smelling. Probably because it never saw the light of day. Sebastian wondered what had gone on behind the walls all those years ago. It amazed him at how easily Cora navigated the narrow flooring.

She led them to a small room, probably one used to hide women and children if the castle were under attack. It was obvious from first glance that this was Cora's hidden room.

"So, this is where you come when you seek solitude..."

"Yes," she replied.

He smiled. "You amaze me."

"Come, we best return before someone misses us," she said.

"But not before we share a kiss," he replied. He took her in his arms and kissed her. He prolonged the kiss as he felt her tremble with excitement. When he did end the kiss, neither of them wanted it to stop.

Silently they walked back along the narrow corridor until she found another hidden opening.

"This one exits into a little-used storage room near the kitchens," she said quietly.

"Won't it look odd if we suddenly appear near the kitchens?"

She shook her head. "No, not at all. Any of the staff will merely think I'm showing you the castle. They're used to my unusual appearances."

They emerged in the storage room and Cora led him out and down the long hall toward another room. When she opened the door, he could see it was done in shades of pink, gold, and white. The furniture all had Holland covers draped over the furniture. Judging from the lack of dust, he concluded the staff still came in here and cleaned on a regular basis, and if he had to guess his conclusion would be that this had been Cora's mother's own private sitting room.

"This was my mother's. I sometimes come here to be alone."

"You have lots of hiding places."

She smiled. "This is the only one anyone knows about. My father knows I come here."

"You must miss her terribly."

"It's been a long time, but yes. I wonder what she would think of how I turned out."

He wrapped his arms around her tightly, instinctively knowing she needed his closeness. "Ah, but that story is far from finished."

"True."

"How would she have taken to your training horses?"

"I imagine she would have accepted it, though not without voicing her opinions on the matter."

"I'm sure."

"She always knew I wasn't the typical girl, that I had interests that far surpassed the usual embroidery and piano," she said.

"You certainly aren't typical, and that's what makes you unique."

She turned to him. "What about you? Your parents?"

"Well, naturally, my father died or else I wouldn't be Duke. He died suddenly while I was away at University. My mother died of a broken heart not long after he did. They were very close."

"I'm sorry."

"No need, I still have my paternal grandmother living. She lives in the dowager house on my estate, still gets around quite well, tends her own small rose garden. Something she would have never been caught doing thirty years ago. Age does change us," he murmured.

"So, she's all alone?"

"She has her lady's maid, who's been with her for as long as I can remember. They're more like friends now, and she has the occasional visitor. The vicar and one or two of the church ladies call on her regularly."

"She sounds amazing. Perhaps I'll meet her one day."

Sebastian knew if he had his way the two women would meet in the not-too-distant future. "I'm sure you will."

She smiled. "I look forward to it. Now, if you'll excuse me, I should get to the stables."

"Time for feeding?"

"No, a little early, but I like to make sure everything is prepared properly for our new guests. You know how delicate Thoroughbreds can be."

"Yes, that they can, though I don't think Apollo will be a bother. He's fairly stout."

She started toward the door. "Would you like to accompany me, Your Grace, or do you have more pressing matters?"

"I don't want to monopolize your time, Lady Cora," he replied with a smile.

"You won't be. I thought you might like to see how we do things while you are here."

"Very well, lead the way."

She led him through the corridors until they came back around to the front door. "It's still a beautiful day, let's take the long way."

He nodded walking beside her. Their relationship had come a long way in such a short time, becoming friends. A long way from the mutual dislike their relationship had started out with. They still sparred, but it had turned good-natured, both knowing what provoked the other. Did they have a chance at a future together? Surprisingly he found himself wanting Cora in his life on a more permanent basis.

14

____

After dinner, the Duke and Sebastian rejoined Cora in the drawing room. Sebastian had been able to speak with the older gentleman while they were having their port. He was relieved that Augustus and his friends had not joined them this evening. It gave him time to get an idea of how the Duke might feel about courting his daughter. He was not disappointed.

"I cannot tell you how delightful it's been to have you here," the Duke said. "I know you leave in a day or two, but I thought if you wanted, we might go hunt in the morning. Early, mind you. There is a place where a certain stag likes to come early in the day."

"I would like that, sir," he replied.

"Excellent." the Duke studied Sebastian for a moment or two. "What's on your mind?"

Sebastian tried not to show surprise. Was it that obvious of his affections for Cora? "I was wanting to speak to you about something, Your Grace."

"Does it have something to do with my daughter?"

Sebastian arched a brow, surprised at how preceptive the older man was. "Yes. I—I would like your permission to court her."

"I see. Does Cora know of your intentions?"

"No. I thought before I pursued it any further with her, I should ask your permission."

The Duke took a thoughtful sip of his port and placed the glass back on the table. "What are your intentions?"

"I would like to marry Cora."

"I see. I don't have to tell you what a handful she can be," he replied.

Sebastian smiled. "Trust me, I do."

"You have my blessing and permission."

"Thank you, Your Grace."

"Enough with the formalities. My only wish is that this is not a long courtship."

"My wish, as well."

The Duke smiled, looking a little misty-eyed. "I've waited for a long time to see this. I'm glad it's you, Hightower."

"I still have to discuss matters with Cora."

"She is going to accept. Whether it's courting or a betrothal, she'll accept. She's quite taken with you."

Sebastian smiled and leaned back in his chair. "After a rocky start."

"Yes," the older man replied with a smile.

"When I return, we'll discuss matters more serious."

"Her dowry."

"I don't need the money. I thought I might put the majority into a trust for any daughters we may have."

"An excellent idea," the Duke replied.

"I thought so. Daughters are usually only provided for in their dowry, and as we know that becomes the property of her husband. I'd like to do something more. In case one doesn't marry."

"I see you've thought this out quite thoroughly."

"I have tried." He finished his port. "I suppose we should rejoin Cora before she comes looking for us."

"Yes," he replied, rising from his chair. "Why don't you take Cora for a turn in the gardens. I'm going to make myself scarce, I have a good book I brought back from London I've yet to get to."

Sebastian rose. "Thank you, Your Grace."

Both men walked back into the drawing room where Cora was sitting in front of the fire, a tea service on the table before her. She looked up, almost relieved to not be left alone any longer. Sebastian had the feeling she disliked this part of being a woman. Being left out of more tantalizing, constructive conversation.

"Did you solve all the world's problems? She teased with a twinkle in her eye.

"Alas, no. Only one or two got our attention," Sebastian replied.

She turned toward her father. "Papa would you care for some tea?"

He shook his head. "No, I think I'm going to retire to my study. There's a novel I purchased in London I've been wanting to start. Why don't you and Sebastian take a turn outside? It's a lovely night, and the moon is still out."

"Very well. If you're sure."

"Yes. Enjoy the rest of your evening." He walked over and kissed Cora on the forehead before quitting the room.

Cora watched him until the door closed behind him before turning her attention to Sebastian. "Your Grace, would you care to see the gardens? Again?"

"I would like that immensely," he replied.

He followed her out to the terrace off the drawing room. Cora explained her grandfather had added the feature in order to make it easier for her grandmother to enjoy her garden. She walked to the wide, gray balustrade and gazed out over the pristine gardens full of roses, peonies, and many other blooms. He was surprised at the different species. Scotland was known for its sometimes-brutal winters, and it amazed him how it reminded him of an English garden. He stood next to her, probably closer than he should, but Sebastian saw no reason for them to pretend there wasn't an attraction between them.

Peering out at the gardens below for a moment or two, neither of them uttering a word. Finally, unable to stand it anymore, Sebastian turned towards her.

"Come, shall we walk?"

"Yes. We'll have more privacy if we do," she replied with a mischievous grin on her face. She looked even more beautiful in the moonlight as it bathed light down on her.

He offered his arm, which she accepted, tucking her hand around the crook of his arm. He led her down the stairs and on to the path.

"Which way?" he asked.

"Either way. They both return here. There are benches we can sit on should you wish to talk, or just enjoy the gardens."

"Lead the way," he replied. He held his breath in anticipation.

Stopping in front of a small fountain, he put his hand on her face, cradling it. His head dipped, stopped as he gazed at her, then lowered again as he kissed her.

She accepted his kisses, succumbing to his power. The kisses more intense, capturing her very essence. He sought to kiss her neck and she angled her head to permit him. She shivered in anticipation.

Kissing the top of her head as he pulled her

dress up. His hand slid between her thighs. He reached between her legs, then pressed up against her most feminine part. She clung to him, gasping. She cried out, calling his name as she reached her pleasure. He removed his hand and wrapped his arms around her.

They stood, her body nestled against his. Neither of them wanting to lose the sensual glory that could only exist between a man and a woman.

"Cora, there is something I wish to discuss with you."

"I am still an innocent, if that's what you're wondering," she said.

"No—I mean, that isn't it."

"What is it, Sebastian?"

"I would like to court you."

She gave no reply for several minutes before loosening her grip on him and gazing up at him. "I would like that. Very much."

"You would?" he blurted out.

"Yes. Of course, you'll need my father's permission."

The corners of his mouth pulled up. "We've already discussed the matter."

"You have?"

"Yes. I wanted to have his consent before I spoke with you, and I wanted to do it before I left."

She gazed up at him. "You do realize I won't be like any other woman you may have courted. I'm fiercely independent."

"One of the things I love about you, and you're beautiful and desirable," he replied with a grin.

He kissed her again on the lips, then her cheek. He pulled her closer, wanting the kiss to linger.

"Come, it's getting chilly. We can talk more over a

brandy if you'd like," she said with a smile. Her lips looked puffy from his kisses, her cheeks flushed.

"I would like that."

She grinned. "I would like more of what we started."

"As would I," he replied. "Soon. I promise."

He offered his arm and they leisurely walked back to the stairs leading to the terrace. She led him up the stairs and back into the drawing room. It was empty except for a fire blazing in the fireplace. He walked over to the sideboard, poured two brandies, and strode over to the divan she was seated on. He handed her one before sitting next to her.

"Papa will be happy to learn I've accepted."

"I'm sure he will," he replied. "It won't be easy being so far apart, but I promise to return as soon as Apollo is ready for his race."

"Six weeks is an awfully long time, but I'm sure it'll pass quickly."

He nodded taking a thoughtful sip of his brandy. "It'll pass before you know it."

"What will you do in London?"

"I have some pressing business matters, and I need to ride out to my estate and see how things are progressing."

"And to check on your grandmother?"

He nodded. "Yes, of course."

She gazed at him longingly. "I'm glad I met you, Sebastian."

"As am I."

A clock chimed on the mantel, causing her to look up. "We should retire. You're going to hunt the stag with Papa, and I've got my usual early day."

After finishing their brandies, they rose and faced each other. The air grew thick with things left unspoken. Desire, lust. Instead, they continued to stare at each other.

She smiled tentatively. "Sebastian, would you kiss me goodnight?"

Butterflies exploded in her stomach, her breath hitched as he took her in his arms and kissed her again. His lips were full and sensual, and she shivered with excitement under his firm hold. Her fingers danced through the hair hanging at the nape of his neck, not wanting the moment to end.

Finally he ended the kiss, releasing her.

"Come, or I won't be able to stop myself."

She let him lead her by the hand out of the drawing room. At the top of the stairs, they shared one last kiss before they parted to each other's respective chambers.

"Good night. I'll see you upon our return," he finally said his eyes still locked with hers.

"Hopefully with the stag."

Watching as he turned and began walking away, her fingers brushed against her kissed swollen lips.

"Good night," she called out.

Sebastian undressed to his smalls and donned a robe. He picked up a book he'd brought along, but the words ran together. Then he heard a light knock on the door. He strode over and opened the oak door, and there stood Cora in her night rail. Her hair was loose, tumbling down her shoulders and back, curls hanging loose. His mouth dried at the sight of her.

He stood aside so she could enter. Slowly she floated past him, strolling around the chamber, her long, elegant fingers running along the furnishings.

"I couldn't sleep," she whispered.

"Did you even try?" he countered.

"Perhaps. All that I can think of is you. Your touch. I want more, Sebastian."

"Are you sure?" he asked. "Because there will be no turning back."

She did not object. "I know."

"I'll lock the door. No one will bother us."

She nodded, and he began to remove her night rail. As he did the whole world disappeared.

He marveled at her as her dressing gown fell to the floor. He embraced her tightly as she responded to his kisses. He held her head as they shared dueling kisses, releasing their mutual passion and desire.

Kissing her neck his hands began caressing her body. She gasped as he suckled her breast. Moments later he was undressing, as he watched her. Naked, he lifted her and carried her to his bed.

Again, he caressed her breasts, dipping his head and letting his tongue flick the tight tip. Her breath hitched as his caresses lowered, exploring between her thighs. She reached out to touch him. Not tonight. Another time. He took her hand and held it above her head. "Not tonight. Tonight is about you," he rasped.

He commanded her with his hands and mouth, and helplessly she lost control, wanting more. She thrashed about as he stroked her and took the pleasure higher. She went over the edge, breathless.

Sebastian covered her, releasing her hands as he filled her. She grasped him wanting more. The feel of her tightness was so right and perfect. He lost himself in her until he felt his seed spilling within her. He felt complete; she made him feel whole.

Contented, their bodies still touched as he gathered her in his arms. He knew a lot about how to pleasure a woman, but his former lovers had never been like Cora.

Feeling his eyes grow heavy, he struggled to stay awake. She seemed to be thinking the same thing. "I should go," she murmured.

"Not yet," he replied softly. He pulled her on top of him and caressed her breasts, her face half obscured by her hair. She looked down at him with glistening green eyes. He reached between her thighs and gently stroked her until she cried out. Lifting her, he entered her slowly.

Cora gazed down at him, looking at how they were joined. "Show me how."

He lifted her, then slid her back down. "Do you like that?"

"Yes. It feels strange, but wonderful."

Afraid he was about to end the game, he felt her quicken her pace. Her eyes were closed as she found her own pleasure with the deep thrusts. She threw her head back, riding him, gasping for more.

Sebastian slid his hand between their bodies and touched her where they joined. She instantly lost control. Cora squirmed against him hard as he pulled her down on him and held her hips. He took control, thrusting long and hard as he climbed to Nirvana.

After she rolled off his muscular body, he gathered her in his arms and held her for several minutes. Finally, he spoke. "That was beyond anything I could have imagined, but I'm afraid you need to go.

"Are you trying to get rid of me?"

"No. I'm afraid we'll fall asleep."

"Yes, we probably will." Kissing him once more, she rolled out of his warm embrace. Standing at the side of his bed, she bent over and picked up her night rail and slid it over her head. Heading to the door, she turned one last time to look at him before opening the door and heading back to her room, her life forever changed.

~

THE FOLLOWING MORNING, Cora returned to the castle after finishing her early morning rides and training. She was pleased with how quickly Apollo was responding to her. She had been right—the colt had been bored and needed someone new. There were a few things she wanted to work on with him, but for now, they were still getting to know each other. Once she and the youngster didn't have Sebastian to distract them, it would be easier to progress his training.

Cora smiled as she thought of the time she and Sebastian had spent the night before. She certainly hadn't intended to ever become involved with him, but the attraction was there, and neither of them could escape its hold. She certainly could do worse than the Duke, and he appeared to be just as he presented himself to be. An honest, caring man, who wouldn't demand she stop her pursuits once they married—or would he? That was non-negotiable. She would never give up training racers, not even for Sebastian. She'd worked too hard to get where she was. Most importantly, her father approved, and he liked Sebastian.

She walked into the drawing room for her usual morning tea. She usually rose early and headed to the stables to begin her day, the only nourishment she might take with her was an oatcake or scone. Anything else waited until her work was done.

Augustus sat sprawled in one of the large, overstuffed chairs near the fire. Her brother rarely rose before noon, so he must want something.

"Good morning," she said.

"Ah, you've obviously been up early riding or whatever it is you do," he replied.

"Papa went hunting."

"So, I heard. With the Duke no less."

"Yes. Papa thought he might like to try hunting here, since he's never been stag hunting."

"He never gives me the time of day, much less goes hunting with me," Augustus sneered.

Cora gazed disapprovingly at her brother. "That's because you've just returned."

"I've been back long enough," he countered.

"Augustus, you've brought friends back with you, you rarely rise before noon, and you're into your cups not long after. Do you really think you could hunt?"

"You know what your problem is, Cora? Papa's been too lenient with you. He allows you to pursue things a lady shouldn't and praises you for it. What you need is a strong, firm hand."

"Since you're not my father nor my guardian, you have no say in the matter," she replied.

"I intend to put a stop to all this foolishness. I know the perfect choice for a husband, and he's staying at my home. I plan to speak with our father about it today."

She arched a brow and smiled. "I'm afraid that won't be necessary, Augustus. Hightower has asked to court me, and Papa has given his consent."

"What? You can't!"

"And why not? Hightower is kind, caring, and has money of his own. He isn't after my dowry, like most of your friends."

"I won't allow it!" Augustus bellowed, his face turning blotched red.

"You have no say in the matter. Should Hightower ask me to become his wife, I will accept, and there is nothing you can do about it. Go home, Augustus. Take some pride in yourself and don't let Papa see you like this."

The butler stood with a footman at the door with the tea tray. Cora immediately walked over towards them. "I'll have my tea in my chambers."

"This is not over, Cora."

"Stay out of my business," she spat before quitting the room.

She made her way upstairs to her room, seething at the audacity of her brother. She knew very good and well why he was trying to force a match with one of his friends. He needed funds and had made a deal with one of them. Marry her, and he got a portion of her dowry.

She needed to speak with both her father and Sebastian when they returned. Augustus wouldn't let go. He was desperate and probably deep in debt. She imagined it wouldn't take much digging to find he had probably gambled away most of his funds, but how bad was it? And where had he spent it? He hadn't been back from the Continent long, or had he? Had he spent it there, on whores or gambling? Probably both.

Cora decided she would have Sebastian make some discreet inquiries when he returned to London. With Augustus in his mood, she hated to see Sebastian go. There had to be a way to make her brother back off, find something else to catch his attention. Perhaps Sebastian would have an idea.

She sat in her small sitting room in front of a fire with her tea, contemplating what her brother's next move might be, and how he could be handled. Her father had already given his blessing for her to court Sebastian and would never be swayed by Augustus.

Until she had answers, she needed to stay out of his way.

"I have your bath drawn, my lady," her lady's maid said from the doorway to her dressing room.

Cora stirred from her thoughts and put down her cup. "Thank you."

She rose and walked toward the dressing room. Her father had installed hot and cold water taps in the castle a few years prior, making it a lot easier for one to take a bath. No longer were a stream of footmen needed to carry water up and down the stairs.

"I think I'll wear the lavender dress today. The one with the gray piping" she said as she passed her maid.

"Very well, my lady."

"The Duke and I are now courting, so I need to look my best when I'm not dressed for the stables."

The maid smiled. "You'll dazzle the Duke when I finish with you. It makes my heart joyful to hear you've finally found a man. His Grace seems to adore you."

"I certainly hope so. He's due to return to London tomorrow – just until his colt is ready to race. He'll be back in about a month."

"He'll be back before you know it, my lady," the maid replied.

"Yes, he will. In the meantime, I'll have to stay vigilant. My brother is not happy with my choice."

"If I may be so bold as to speak out of turn, my lady?"

A thin smile crossed Cora's lips. "Of course."

"Your brother is unhappy with your choice because your choice isn't one he wants."

Cora nodded. "Yes, Augustus is not the same man who left here two years ago."

"He was a boy when he left, my lady. He returns as a broken, unhappy, and angry man."

"And I refuse to allow him to try and control my life."

"Is His Grace Hightower aware of your brother's motives?"

"He is," Cora replied, this time with a grin on her face.

Her maid smiled and bobbed her head.

For now, she would keep herself busy and advise her father what she'd learned and wait for Sebastian to return.

15

Cora kept herself busy after Sebastian left. Her charges kept her mornings busy, exercising and training. She loved nothing more than working with a horse who had problems or starting a green youngster —she loved everything about her business. The road had been long and hard, and she wouldn't change a thing. Apollo was coming along nicely, and she couldn't wait for Sebastian to see the results.

Augustus and his friends had been keeping to themselves, and her obnoxious brother hadn't been seen in days. Not since their father admonished him for his behavior. Still, Cora didn't trust him.

A late morning rainstorm kept her from her usual ride. She rode a sturdy bay gelding who'd recently been retired from his usual duties. He'd been both a riding and coach horse, mainly for the cart and farm implements. He still had a lot of spunk left in him, and no one could see just putting him out in the pasture for his remaining days. She rode him a couple of days a week, until she and the stable manager could decide where he'd best fit now.

Cora decided to go out to the small lake to give her mount a rest while she relaxed and made plans. As she neared a cleared-out area where she and her family often came to for picnics, she noted her brother's young stallion. He was flashy, shiny black, with two alternating white stockings and a star and a snip on his face. It had been one he'd purchased from a friend of his, though Cora had his doubts as to how the animal had actually been purchased.

Augustus was seated on a wood bench their father had recently replaced. It was where their mother had sat often, watching as her husband and children fished and played at the water's edge. Those had been memorable times. Everything changed after their mother died of a respiratory illness. In three short years she had gone from a vivacious, fun-loving woman with gleaming red hair, to a much thinner, quieter version of herself, still in her thirties. Her death was a horrible time for the family. She and Augustus were sent to Aunt Henrietta.

She slowly approached. At first Augustus didn't seem to notice her. Cora watched as he scrubbed his face with his hands. Had those been tears she thought she saw? If so, why?

She quietly grew near before stopping the gelding. She dismounted, tied her mount to a small nearby tree and walked towards her brother. He glanced in her direction and shook his head.

"What brings you all the way over here?" Cora asked. "I know you have a lake on your own estate."

"I prefer this one," he replied.

"Yes, it holds a lot of wonderful memories, doesn't it?"

He nodded, not looking at her, but instead staring out across the lake. "It does," he finally said.

"Is something troubling you, Augustus? You haven't been yourself since you've returned."

"It's not something I should burden you with."

"I'm a lot stronger than you're giving me credit for," she murmured. "Where are your friends?"

"Gone."

"Really? I thought they were here for a while."

Augustus shook his head and gazed at her. "Actually, we had a falling-out of sorts."

"Do you want to tell me about it, or should I guess? I wouldn't accept either of them for a husband, and that angered one or both. Am I close?"

He blew out a sigh. "Yes, but there's more to it than just that."

"You know you can tell me. It won't go any further. You know that."

"I know. I just don't know where to begin."

She arched a brow. "Are you in trouble, Augustus?"

He said nothing for a moment, not until she took his hand and squeezed it like she used to when they were children. "I owe some money."

"Gambling?"

He nodded. "Yes. It was more than I can access without arousing suspicions of our solicitors."

"To your friends. I take it my dowry would have been used as repayment?"

"Yes, and I would have profited as well," he replied quietly. "Since you refused both of them, they called in my debt."

"Oh, Augustus! What now? Where will you get the funds?"

"That's not your problem, dear Cora. It's my mess, and I must clean it up."

"Why not go to Papa? I'm sure if you explained, he'd forgive you and let you borrow against your trust."

They had both been left a trust by their mother,

but neither could come into it without their father's signature until they were thirty. Augustus still had two years.

"I can't disappoint him like that."

"May I ask how much you owe them?"

"Ten thousand pounds."

Cora looked at him in disbelief. This was a substantial amount for anyone. "What are you going to do? Your estate is entailed so they can't touch that."

"By the grace of God. They left with my carriage, team, and stallion at an agreed-upon price. Not that it makes a dent in the balance."

"You know Papa's going to find out. Word will get back to him just about the fact your carriage, team, and horse are gone."

He pulled a flask out of his coat pocket and handed it to her. She shook her head and watched as Augustus took a healthy drink.

"Things got out of hand while I was on the Continent. Now I'm paying for it."

She stared at him for a moment. "Is that whiskey from your stills?"

"Aye, it is. Unfortunately, I only have a dozen barrels left of that particular year, and I can't afford to run the distillery on my own without Papa's money, thanks to this mess I've gotten myself into. I'm grateful he's kept it running."

"I may have a solution—an idea that may help you."

"What sort of idea?"

She smiled slyly. "I need to think one through, but they both may work."

"Tell me."

"Aunt Henrietta is due in a matter of days. She adores you, Augustus. Why not approach her about a loan. A loan to invest in the distillery. You know she'd never tell Papa, and it could work until I can formulate my plan for the other idea."

"I don't know. She'll ask why I don't do the same with our solicitors and get a loan against my trust."

Cora shook her head of dark hair. "No, she won't. Plus, you know Auntie's tasted your single-malt. You gifted her with a barrel before you left for the Continent."

"I'd forgotten about that. It was a barrel of the ten-year-old. My first batch."

"For now, you could buy the grain you need and make your first batch, separate from what Papa's making. Your whiskey is among the finest, so why not use your skills and make money from it?"

"That will help, but what do I do to repay the debt?"

"I told you I have an idea, but it may take a couple of weeks to put together."

"Very well," he replied, nodding. "When Aunt Henrietta arrives, I will speak with her about a loan for the distillery. I'll leave the rest to you and hope they don't start making demands."

"Excellent."

Cora hated to see her brother in this predicament but was relieved he'd seen his friends were not the upstanding young men he thought them to be. She hoped he'd learned from his mistakes. This evening she would write Sebastian, explaining the situation and her solutions. She had a solution to her brother's problem, but it would have to involve Sebastian. She knew him well enough to know he wouldn't agree to anything unless there was something in it for him. He was a businessman, a good one, and one she respected.

"You're happy with this Duke?"

"Yes, immensely."

He smiled. "He's not going to force you to give up your horse training, is he?"

"Absolutely not. It's my business, and I won't give it up for him or any other man. If there's one thing Hightower knows about me, it's that I'm stubborn. If it creates conflict, Sebastian and I will work it out. We always do."

"How and where will you continue?" he asked.

"I don't know. We haven't really talked about it. He has a country home, so I imagine that's where I'll move it."

"I hope for your sake you'll be happy and successful."

"He hasn't asked to marry me," she said smiling.

"He's smitten with you, Cora. It's only a matter of time. He isn't going to stand for a long-distance courtship."

"I expect when he returns in a few weeks, he will ask Papa's permission for us to become betrothed and married," she replied.

"I wish only the best for you, and I apologize for being the way I was.

This was more like the Augustus she grew up with. For the first time since he'd returned, the bond they had shared before he left was resurfacing.

"Apology accepted. Just do me a favor and choose your friends a little more wisely? And no more gambling."

He rose from the bench and extended his hand. "You don't have to worry about either. Now, would you fancy a ride?"

She let him hold her horse as she mounted. Once he was ready, they headed towards a large meadow they had raced across as children. Cora pulled away from him and urged the gelding into a gallop, leaving Augustus behind her. She knew her horse didn't have a chance against his powerful stallion but galloped the beast as fast as he could muster. Moments later, Augustus's stallion passed them as though they were standing still. Just like he did in years gone by.

Tonight she would write to Sebastian and get his thoughts on what Augustus had told her. He could check into the matter without raising her brother's suspicions. She didn't doubt what he told her, but she needed to be sure. Was this sudden change all he told her, or was he setting her up for something else?

FOR THE SECOND TIME, Sebastian reread Cora's letter, which had arrived at his London home this morning. It was slightly distressing. She'd told him of her brother's sudden reverse in attitude, and how she'd found him at the lake at their family home. Cora mentioned Augustus's confession, and the gambling debts. She outlined how her brother had given up his prized carriage-and-four to go towards repayment, but it was not nearly enough. When she mentioned the staggering amount Augustus owed, his fist balled. How could he have been so reckless?

He smiled when he reached the part where Cora wrote of her idea for her brother to retake his place at the distillery. One idea was that he would ask their aunt for a loan. She saw no reason why their aunt wouldn't lend him the capital for him to invest in the distillery. She and Augustus both had a trust left by their mother, but until they were thirty, neither could access funds unless they petitioned the solicitors.

Their aunt could help with the capital, and Augustus could repay it as soon as the solicitors granted him money from his trust.

The operation was on their family estate, which would one day be his. Obviously, their father had not objected to his son being in the whiskey business. It brought jobs, and a steady income for Augustus, and therefore the Dukedom.

Cora had obviously thought this through with great care. She wanted to help her brother and asking for his opinion and suggestions. She was like that, caring, though she mentioned that she sincerely hoped this was not some elaborate ruse her brother might have come up with, in an attempt to marry her off to one of his friends to settle his debt. Marry her to the friend to whom he owed the sum. Even though his friends had left, Cora had a bad feeling about it all.

Sebastian sucked in a breath, trying to keep his temper in check. He was not about to let that happen. Her father didn't care for either of his son's friends to begin with, and the discussions he and the Duke had had were productive. Not only that, but the older man had been agreeable when Sebastian had spoken of marriage to Cora.

Further down in her letter, she was telling him how much she missed him and how well Apollo was responding to training. She was certain he'd be ready for the Scottish race. He was doing that well. He felt heat flow through his body as she described in muted detail what she wanted from him when he returned. His cock was going places it shouldn't, but as Sebastian well knew, he couldn't always control his desires.

He sighed and took out paper and a pen, but first he needed to think this through. He had almost caught up with any pressing matters that brought him back to London. His sisters were occupied, so they wouldn't notice he was gone. They were used to him having to travel extensively for both his ducal duties and his businesses.

His butler, James, appeared before him. "I'm sorry to disturb you Your Grace. The Earl of Yorkshire is here and is requesting to see you. I told him you didn't wish to be disturbed, but he insisted I let you know of his arrival."

Allgood was persistent. He wouldn't take no for an answer, and quite frankly Sebastian thought it might be good to speak with someone about Cora's letters. The one pertaining to her brother.

He sighed and sat back in his chair. "Show him in."

The butler arched a brow, said nothing and left the room to find Allgood, not that his friend would wait.

Allgood came bursting through the door and plopped himself in his usual seat in front of Sebastian's desk.

"Ye gads, man. You've been nothing but a bore since you returned from Scotland. I'm here to relieve you of whatever it might be you think is so important."

"I have obligations, Crispin."

"We all do, but they don't consume our days. You need to come with me for a ride in the park. You need to be seen by all the eligible young ladies and their mamas."

Sebastian shook his head. "No, I don't."

"How do you expect to find a wife sitting inside in this dreary old study?"

"I've already found her."

Allgood leaned forward and poured himself a healthy splash of whiskey from a decanter Sebastian kept on the corner of his desk. "Do tell. Who is she?"

"Lady Cora Keats, the Duke of Dover's daughter."

His friend whistled softly, smiled, and took a drink of his whiskey. "Does the lady know? I thought the two of you were mortal enemies."

"Yes, of course she knows. I have spoken with her father, the Duke, and have his permission to court her."

"But?"

"But nothing. When I return to Scotland to pick up Apollo's Gold, I will ask for her hand. Something her father and I also discussed, and he's unopposed to."

"This is quick. You haven't ruined her have you?"

Sebastian curbed his temper. He and Allgood had been friends far too many years. He knew his friend's odd sense of humor, and this was one of them. "Bite your tongue. That is none of your business."

"I see. Will she be happy living here in England, you think?"

"Yes," he replied. "There is something I would like to discuss with you. Something I may need your help with."

Allgood downed his whiskey and sat back in his chair. "Now you have me most curious."

For the next ten minutes Sebastian spoke, telling his friend details of what Cora had written to him about. Her brother's friends, his gambling debt, and his sudden change in behavior.

"You need to find out more on these two friends of her brother's. I know someone who can help with that."

Sebastian smiled. "I knew you would. I would also like to look into her brother. Discreetly, of course."

"What exactly are you looking for?"

"His business dealings. Lady Cora says he's going to resume his position at the distillery and make whiskey once again. I want to know everything there is to know on him."

"You'll want to know if he's still in touch with his two friends?"

"Yes. He was determined Lady Cora marry one of them. Something changed that made them leave without either of them pursuing her."

Allgood arched a brow. "Don't you think they merely gave up and left when they saw they were going to get nowhere with Lady Cora?"

"With her brother's gambling debts? No. She was his way to repay them. There's more than he's telling Lady Cora."

"Anything else?"

"I want to know all there is to know about this distillery."

"Why? Is he looking for investors, or just a loan to help him? Allgood asked. "You aren't thinking of investing, are you?"

"Perhaps, but first I need to know the distillery's reputation and quality of the whiskey he was producing."

"You need to see the books if you're serious," Allgood replied.

"I know that. My first concern is finding out the validity of her brother's sudden change of attitude. Is he sincere or is this something much more sinister?

"I'll get on it as soon as I leave here. I should have some answers quickly."

"Excellent."

Allgood cracked a smile. "From mortal enemies to lovers. I must admit I never saw that coming."

"Nor I."

"I think she's good for you, from what I know of her. Tell me, will you be living here or in Scotland?"

"We'll reside at Hightower Hall of course," he replied, adding, "I plan on moving her training operation there. I'll have a track built, as well as a separate stable."

"So you're going to let her continue training racehorses?"

Sebastian sat back in his chair and studied his friend for a moment. "Yes. I can think of no reason why she can't carry on, and she certainly isn't going to quit because I tell her to. I will support her for as long as she wishes to continue."

"You know that means all of polite society will know of her unconventional hobby."

"It's not a hobby and bugger them all."

"You say that now, but it may be something entirely different, once gentlemen find out the trainer they've been sending their prized horses to is a woman. You know some men's opinions on women. They aren't going to like it, and it could affect her father as well."

"You're telling me I need to curtail her activities?"

"I'm saying, go slow. I'm sure Lady Cora will agree, since she knows first-hand," he said.

"Point taken. This will be something we need to work out. I was only thinking of her happiness. I'd forgotten the ramifications it all could have, but knowing Cora, she isn't going to budge. She's worked too hard to earn her reputation. She's worked too hard to give it up."

"Aren't you glad I stopped by?" Allgood gloated.

"I am."

"I'll look into things for you," he said. "Could I interest you in lunch? You really need to get out of this house."

"You're right. I've been at this desk far too long. Lunch it is."

With Allgood using his resources to investigate Augustus's two friends, Sebastian knew he could breathe a little easier. He wouldn't be sitting in London waiting. He would head back to Scotland by the first of the week, giving him time to tie up any loose business.

16

Sebastian arrived in Scotland on a cold, rainy afternoon. He descended the carriage and ran past a waiting footman holding an umbrella and through the front door. Quickly he removed his greatcoat, gloves, and hat, and handed them to the butler. No one was around to greet him, making him wonder for a moment if his correspondence had reached Scotland.

"Would you care to freshen up first, Your Grace? I readied the same rooms you occupied last time you visited."

"Is no one home?" Sebastian countered.

"His Grace is in his study and Lady Cora and her aunt, Lady Henrietta, went to the village. At her aunt's insistence, if I might add."

He smiled at the thought of Cora being dragged from shop to shop with her aging aunt. The visit to the village meant taking her away from her training and horses. Her aunt was probably aware of the fact and was using it to her advantage. Cora mentioned her aunt strongly disapproved of her pursuits. Young ladies were supposed to be finding a suitable match, getting married, and having children. In their spare time, her aunt thought she should be practicing the piano or harp and doing needlework. Not astride powerful horses.

"I believe I'll freshen up first if you'd inform His Grace of my arrival. Tell him I'll join him in his study in thirty minutes."

"Very well, Your Grace."

Sebastian ascended the stairs two at a time. He easily found his rooms and found Titus unpacking and laying out a change of clothes.

"Good man," he murmured. Titus seemed to always know his needs, sometimes before he even did.

"Will there be anything else, Your Grace?" Titus asked, as he finished tying Sebastian's cravat.

"No. I'm meeting with the Duke. Keep your ears open, see what's been going on while we've been away."

Titus nodded, understanding what Sebastian wanted, but then he always did. He could blend in and find out things Sebastian might never hear about.

Sebastian headed back downstairs to the Duke's study. A footman stood outside and quickly announced his arrival.

"Hightower, I hope you had a decent journey despite the weather," the older man said, standing. He motioned to a high-back leather chair in front of the fire. "Come, let's sit over here."

He followed the Duke over to the hearth and sat down while Cora's father walked over to a decanter. "Would you care to try what's being made at our distillery? This one's five years old, so Augustus oversaw it."

"Very much. I understand Augustus has quite a knack for making whiskey."

"Aye, he does, though he abandoned it when he

went to the Continent with his friends. I've managed to keep it going with the help of a good man."

"How much are you producing?" Sebastian asked, as he accepted the glass.

"Nowhere near what we once did. Augustus was turning it into a profitable business."

Sebastian swirled the amber liquid and took a swallow. It was rich, full-bodied. Not overly powerful or biting like some. "I understand he's wanting to get back into it."

"He is, but he's going to have to prove himself."

"That is only fair," Sebastian replied.

"He's decided he wants back in at the distillery and wants to increase production."

"You grow your own barley?"

"Yes, Augustus's estate does well enough producing the grain, but it could do better."

"Sounds like what he needs is a good distribution line."

"Aye. Right now it's with a select few. Those who've bought from us for years."

Sebastian took another swallow and glanced at the older man. "Has your estate always produced single-malt?"

He nodded. "Aye. The only time we haven't was after Culloden. No one did. Or if you did, you kept it well hidden."

"I understand. The whiskey is good, one of the best I've tasted."

"Thank you."

Sebastian set his glass down on a table next to him. "If you'd like, I could speak with several friends of mine about taking the brand on. One distributes to high-end establishments in London, and the other two are located around major cities in the north."

"I couldn't ask such a favor."

"You didn't. I offered."

The older duke arched a silver brow. "Why would you do that?"

They both drank. "My idea might help Augustus get on track again."

"What's your idea?"

This time Sebastian took a thoughtful sip of his whiskey. "I want to invest in the distillery. I understand it is ultimately your business, but that you've left the operations to Augustus, and we both know how that's turned out."

"You've obviously got a plan in mind."

"I do. I invest enough money to grow the distillery. I'll speak with my contacts about distribution in London. I will pay off Augustus's debts. I understand you and he split the profits fifty-fifty, and I will uphold your fifty percent. In return, Augustus will see only ten percent of his portion of the profits until I am repaid. Until then, my portion will be forty percent. Once I've been repaid, I will become a silent partner and will only ask for a smaller portion of the profits and have access to the books once a quarter. The details to that will be worked out."

"That's more than generous, Hightower. My only concern is Augustus. He might say he's given up his habits, but who's to say he's only full of talk. Then what do we do?"

"That is a decision we'll need to decide, either now or later. Ultimately the distillery is yours as duke. It employs a good many people in the area and I believe we can set up enough safeguards to protect the distillery from Augustus's ruin."

"Hire a man to oversee it, like is done now?"

"Yes. Does anyone come to mind?"

"Liam MacRae comes to mind. He's been at the job for ten years. He's kept the distillery afloat despite Augustus's actions. His father did the job before him, so he it's in his blood."

"Good, I'd like to meet with him. If we're in agreement, I'll have my solicitors draw up the necessary paperwork. After we present this to Augustus, of course."

Dover nodded and finished off his whiskey. "Allow me to think all this over before I commit."

"Of course. I realize it's a lot to take in."

"Aye, it is, but it would remedy a lot of things. I'm not sure how Augustus will take to the idea."

"The only way to find out is to present the idea to him."

Sebastian saw a way to tell the man his intentions regarding his daughter. "There is something else I would like to discuss with you, Your Grace."

"Would it have something to do with Cora?"

"I love Cora. I wish to offer for her. I want to marry her... with your permission of course."

Sebastian held his breath waiting for the Duke's answer.

"Yes, you are just who Cora needs. You have my permission and my blessing. We can go over the paperwork in the morning."

"Thank you, Your Grace. I promise she'll be happy."

Dover chuckled. "You'll be the one to bear her wrath if she isn't."

Sebastian smiled and watched as the older man rose from his chair and pick up the decanter of whiskey. He walked back and poured them both a healthy splash. He handed the glass to Sebastian.

"Here's to you and Cora."

The two men enjoyed another splash of whiskey in silence.

"Go find Cora. I know she's learned of your arrival and is probably pacing the floor, wondering what we're doing in here."

Sebastian grinned. "I'm sure she is."

"You'll probably find her in the drawing room," Dover said.

Sebastian left the Duke's study feeling like he'd accomplished what he'd set out to do. Cora's father had been receptive and welcoming to both matters. Agreeing to his daughter marriage and being quite interested in what he'd suggested regarding Augustus's debt and the future of the distillery.

He found Cora in the drawing room as the Duke had told him. The butler had just delivered a tea tray, and she was fussing over it, readying to pour herself a cup. She glanced up, smiling as he approached. "Tea? One lump, no milk?"

"Yes, please."

"Were you meeting with Papa?" she asked, as she poured the second cup and handed it off to him. "I hope it went well." She smiled.

He nodded and sat down on a couch in front of the fire. "It did."

"Good."

"How is Apollo?" he asked with a lopsided grin. He knew how badly she wanted to know what the two of them had discussed, but he wasn't going to divulge everything just yet.

Indeed, she did appear flustered by his question. "He's progressing quite nicely. The race is in a fortnight. You'll be staying of course, like we discussed."

"I wouldn't miss it."

She took a sip of tea and set it on the table nearest her. "I'm so glad you're here."

"As am I. Pity we can't enjoy a stroll in the gardens this afternoon."

She cocked her head. "I didn't know you enjoyed gardens so much, Your Grace."

"I've been known to sit in mine and read."

"Did I mention my aunt is here visiting?"

He nodded. "No, but your father did."

"She's lying down. She gets up at dawn, hours before the rest of us, therefore she requires a nap in the afternoon."

"I see. Are you spending time with her?"

"Some. She adores Augustus, and the two of them can be thick as thieves."

He took another sip of tea before setting his cup down. "Speaking of Augustus, I think I may have come up with a solution to help him out. Rid him of his debts, for one. Your father and I discussed it in some detail."

"Oh dear."

"What? What is it?" he asked taking her hand.

"Augustus was going to ask our aunt for a loan to pay off his debts."

"He doesn't need to do that. I told your father I'd be willing to pay off his debts and help acquire some lucrative distributors in London and the north for the distillery. I believe it could become quite profitable, with the right men in place."

"I see. Augustus wouldn't be one of them, would he?"

"He would be involved, but not in the day-to-day operation. We'd continue to use the man in place. Augustus would be a great asset traveling to visit establishments to convince them to purchase the whiskey."

"Wouldn't the distributors do that?"

"They would, but it is always better if someone directly connected with an operation handles some of that. He knows the product probably better than most."

"What do you get in return?"

"It still has to be worked out, but once my loan to your brother has been repaid, I would step back and become more of a silent partner, receiving a much smaller portion of the profits."

He watched her as she thought this through. If it had been any other woman but Cora, he'd never go into detail with her. Cora wasn't like any other woman. She was smart and interested in things most women disdained.

"Augustus would be a fool not to accept it. I know Papa's wanted to grow the distillery. This would be a perfect opportunity to fulfill his dreams."

"I'm glad you agree," he said.

"I understand the distillery is part of the ducal estate. What would happen to it if something were to happen to my father? Augustus would be the Duke. What if he decides not to honor Papa's agreement?"

"Your father and I would make sure that it's taken care of in our paperwork. Not something you should worry yourself about."

"Well, now we wait," she said. "Biscuit? Cook made some shortbread and tarts I forgot to offer when you walked in."

"Yes, and more tea, please."

She rose and glided toward the tea tray. He turned and watched as she prepared a small plate of biscuits and poured two new cups of tea.

Sebastian put the cup on the table in front of him and gazed at Cora. He moved closer and kissed her. "You have no idea how much I've missed this."

"Me too."

He cleared his throat, nervous of what he was going to ask. They had discussed the matter, but nothing could compare to asking her to be his wife.

"Cora, I know we haven't been courting long, but I've found I've fallen in love with you. I want to spend the rest of my life with you. I want you to be my duchess," he said. "Cora, would you do me the honor and become my wife?"

Her answer came before he finished asking. "Yes, Sebastian. Yes!"

~

CORA NEVER EXPECTED to find a man who would accept her for who she was, but here she was, betrothed to the most perfect man in the world. Not only had she thought she'd never marry, but never thought that a peer would find her and her independence refreshing. Surprisingly, she'd found that in a Duke, no less, the Duke of Hightower. She would be a duchess just like her mother, but unlike her mother, Cora knew her life would be vastly different. She would tend to her duties as duchess and mistress of her household, but she would continue her passion of training racehorses.

Cora watched as he pulled a small box out of his pocket. He opened it and took out the most magnificent deep-red ruby ring she'd ever seen.

"This was my grandmother's, and then my mother's. It's only fitting that I pass it along to my duchess," he said, as he took her hand and placed it on her finger.

"It's beautiful, Sebastian."

The edges of his mouth turned up. "Made only more beautiful by the woman whose finger it sits upon."

"Sebastian..."

"We have a wedding to plan, and the sooner the better," he said.

"I don't want anything large or pretentious, unless you do. I'd rather it just be family and perhaps a few close friends."

"If I don't have my sisters in attendance, I'll never hear the end of it."

"We'll pick out a date and you can write your sisters with our news."

He arched a brow. "They'll love any excuse to journey to Scotland."

Cora gazed down at her ring. "We'll speak with Papa this evening. He'll agree with whatever we decide."

"I'm sure he will."

"Apollo will race in a fortnight, and he's more than ready."

"I knew he would be. Something else we need to discuss," he said.

"What's that?"

"Transporting the horses to my estate once we're married."

"Yes, we need to discuss that. Moving them is going to affect more than just me."

"Such as?"

She picked up a cup of cooling tea. "My stablemaster, people who depend on working here. I'm sure my father will find them a place."

There was so much at stake. Cora hadn't realized until now how many people were dependent on her training operation. Moving the horses to England would require a coordinated effort. A track would need to be built, stables too, if Sebastian's weren't large enough.

"We don't have to figure everything out today."

She nodded and smiled. "No, we don't. We could make a list of everyone affected by this, along with what needs to be done to move the operation."

"Excellent idea, sweet. But first I think I need to kiss you. I'm going to burst if I don't."

Cora laughed softly, putting her cup back on the table and stood up. "We can't have that. Come here."

He rose from his place and met her in front of the hearth. Gathering her in his arms Sebastian's lips met hers. The kiss was instantly a desperate, needy, lustful one. She had forgotten how much she'd missed his touch, and intimate exchanges like this.

"Come to me tonight," she whispered in his ear as their kiss ended.

"Yes."

"I've missed you so much, Sebastian. I need you."

"You have no idea how much I've missed you." As though to prove it, he pressed his engorged cock against her.

Cora placed her hand between them and covered his cock. "You have, haven't you."

"Cora..." he rasped.

"We'll have to take care of that tonight," she whispered.

He kissed her again before loosening his embrace. "Come, someone might walk in."

"Sebastian, I had no idea you were so shy," she teased.

A deep rumbling came from deep within his throat. "I don't particularly want you father or aunt to walk in on us. If it weren't for them, I would take you on that chair right now."

"You wouldn't!"

"Ah, but I would."

"We need to wait. There is much to discuss."

He arched his brow and smiled. "Indeed we do. Where would you like to start?"

"My training. I will need a track built on your estate," she said, adding, "I am going to continue my training efforts, and I won't give it up under any circumstances. I've worked long and hard to establish my business."

"I had no doubts you would."

"But?"

"You will be a duchess, and there will be times when your duties are going to have you occupied, or even away."

She ran her hand along his forearm. "I can handle both. Another thought has occurred to me. People might be suspicious when suddenly the Duke of Dover's trainer moves from Scotland to the English countryside."

"Or what are we going to do once people realize the trainer is a woman, and a duchess?"

"Times are changing, Sebastian. Women occupy many jobs once considered only suitable for men. You know I couldn't give a fig about what others think. My title should have no bearing on any of it."

"True."

"And Sebastian? You need to get used to the fact that my training comes first. I'll gladly play hostess, attend societal affairs, but first and foremost, I have my own business to run."

"You drive a hard bargain, but I accept your terms."

"Did I tell you Apollo is doing very well. I can't wait for you to see him run."

"I'm looking forward to it. I knew I made the right decision sending him to you."

"Tell me about Hightower Hall," she said.

"It is where I spent most of my childhood, where I grew up with my sisters. It's been in my family for generations."

"It's in Warwickshire, am I correct?"

"Yes. I also have smaller estates outside Bristol and Cambridge."

"And your townhome in London."

"Correct. All have been part of the Dukedom for years. I visit the other two at least once a year. The townhome is used periodically all year."

"I would like to accompany you when you visit the other two. Who knows, we might want to spend time in Bristol and possibly Cambridge?"

"I thought when we leave here after the wedding, we'd spend a few days in Cambridge before continuing to Hightower Hall."

"I'd like that."

He leaned over and kissed her cheek. "Again, much to discuss."

"Yes. Contacting your sisters is the most important."

"I thought I'd also write Allgood and see if he and his countess might come to our wedding."

"He'd stand up with you?"

Sebastian grinned. "As much as he's been after me to marry, I doubt anything could keep him away."

"Then he must attend."

Cora's mind was whirling. There were so many

things to be done, but she knew they would get everything in place.

17

The evening was a festive affair, as Sebastian and Cora announced their betrothal to Augustus, Aunt Henrietta, and of course, Cora's father, who beamed with pride at his daughter's choice of a husband. Both Augustus and their aunt begrudgingly congratulated them.

Before going into dinner, champagne was served to toast the couple. Naturally, everyone had questions for them. Mainly when the wedding would occur and where would they live.

"It won't be the same with you living so far away," Augustus said, after he offered a toast to the happy couple.

"It's not as far as it once was, thanks to the railroad," Sebastian replied. "You will all have to visit once we've settled in."

Cora nodded. "Yes, all of you."

"We may not have the stags and such, but there's enough game to make a good hunt."

The butler announced dinner, and they all went into the dining room. The meal was special, in honor of Cora and Sebastian's betrothal. The happy couple sat to the Duke's left and right, while Henrietta and Augustus sat next to them.

Sebastian had been paired with Cora and Augustus's aunt. Cora had told him she doted on Augustus, even though she'd never admit it. He also got a sense she was not overly fond of Englishmen. She'd been cold and aloof with him when speaking directly to him, but in the company of others was sparkling and gracious.

What he wasn't expecting was the announcement Augustus and Henrietta decided to make. The pair kept glancing at each other as though sharing a secret. Finally, once the main course of roast duck had been served, Augustus tapped on his wine glass to get everyone's attention.

"I, too, have some exciting news to share," he said as he rose from his chair. "Henrietta is going to invest in the distillery, thus becoming a partner."

Cora's father, Cora, and he all glanced at the other, as the Duke shook his head. Sebastian wondered if by chance the older man had already spoken to his son about Sebastian's offer. It was hard to tell.

Cora countered his news. "That's wonderful because I believe Sebastian is wanting to do the same. The distillery is going to become one of Scotland's finest."

The older woman sniffed. "That really won't be necessary, Your Grace. What I've offered is more than enough."

Before Sebastian could answer, the Duke voiced his opinion. "May I remind you, Augustus, the distillery is still mine. I've tried to overlook your indiscretions while you let the business slip away. As long as I'm still alive, the business will operate as I see fit."

"You're overreacting Papa. Aunt Henrietta has graciously..."

"I know what she's doing," he interrupted. "You either accept the terms Hightower and I have laid out, or I relieve you of all your interest in the distillery, effective immediately. When I am gone, you can do as you see fit."

"You can't do that!" Augustus sputtered.

"I can and I shall." He turned to his sister-in-law. "I've had enough with your meddling and pitting my children against each other. If you want to give Augustus funds, that is your business, but it will not be put into my businesses."

"Then Augustus will open his own. A rival to yours," she said.

"I find your timing questionable, Henrietta."

"And I find your consenting to this marriage questionable."

"Cora's betrothal has nothing to do with the distillery or Augustus. His Grace offered to invest to help grow the distillery. You've made it into a contest, as usual. It won't work."

"I would be a silent partner, Lady Henrietta. Nothing more."

"Well, you and Cora have destroyed that for Augustus, haven't you?"

Sebastian had been afraid something like this would happen if he hadn't had a chance to discuss things privately with Cora's brother. Now their aunt had taken the matter into her own hands, only to have it backfire for her.

"I meant no harm."

The Duke rose from his chair. "This is supposed to be an evening to celebrate Cora and Sebastian. All further discussion on anything else will wait for another time. Right now, I'd like to hear their plans."

"Hightower is going to write his oldest sister and tell her the news. They'll be traveling to Scotland for the wedding," Cora said.

Her father nodded. "Do you have a date yet?"

Sebastian glanced at his betrothed. "We were thinking two days after the race. That gives a fortnight for my sisters and my friend the Earl of Yorkshire to arrive."

The Duke nodded. "Excellent."

"We don't wish this to be a grand affair, Papa. Just you, Augustus, and Aunt Henrietta, along with Hightower's friend and sisters."

"Then the wedding breakfast shall be the grand affair," he said.

Cora glanced at Sebastian. "We thought of marrying in the chapel, if you have no objections."

"Of course I have no objections, but you might be sure your betrothed has no objections to marrying in a Scottish kirk," he smiled.

"No, I don't," Sebastian said. "Perhaps in the morning we could take a walk and look at it."

"I can send word to the vicar to come pay a visit. He could meet you here or at the chapel," the Duke added. "If you'd like, of course."

"Of course," Cora replied with a smile.

"By all means. Have the vicar meet us at the chapel, late morning if possible."

"I'll send word immediately."

The remainder of the evening was pleasant, though rather strained after the incident at the dinner table. Sebastian hoped for Cora's sake everyone came around and shared in her happiness. Much was at stake and a lot would be changing, especially for Cora, and the last thing he wished for her was family discord.

Later that evening, in the privacy of his chamber, Sebastian wrote a letter to Beatrice, telling her the news and inviting his sisters to come to Scotland for the wedding. He skipped most details, only relaying the happy news and the date when the wedding would take place. He urged her to respond immediately and give him their approximate arrival and how they would be traveling.

He handed the letter off to Titus, who was fluttering about the dressing room, making sure everything was as neat as it possibly could be.

"This needs to go out first thing in the morning. It's urgent and needs to reach my sister as quickly as possible."

"No worry, Your Grace. I'll take care of it."

Sebastian watched as his majordomo disappeared. He began to ready himself for bed, excited to see what tomorrow would bring.

～

CORA ROSE EARLY the next morning like she always did, but today was different somehow. She and Sebastian would begin planning not only their wedding, but their future. So many thoughts had run through her head during the night, she barely slept.

This morning she needed to focus all her attentions on to her clients. Soon she would have none. At least temporarily. There was no way she could possibly give any of her clients' horses proper attention with all that she had coming up. She would suspend operations until after she was settled at Hightower Hall. A track would have to be built, and though Sebastian said his stables were adequate and roomy enough for her clients' horses, she would wait and see for herself.

And there was a wedding to plan. Something small, since it would be only family attending. She still wanted everything perfect. Sebastian's sisters would be traveling to Scotland, and she wanted to present a perfect picture once they arrived. The race would be two days after they arrived, and the wedding two days after that. Apart from that, she had no idea what the girls would want to do and suspected she and Sebastian would be staying on for a fortnight in order to let the girls see the Highlands before they left.

18

The whirlwind that was Beatrice, Theodora, and Matilda arrived at Glen Skye Manor early one afternoon. With them came an extra carriage, specifically for their luggage. Cora observed the trio as they stepped from their carriage, taking in the castle before entering, where they would be met by Aunt Henrietta. Her aunt insisted she be the one to greet Sebastian's sisters, commenting that Cora needed to bathe and make herself as presentable as though she were being introduced to royalty. These three young ladies were, after all, to become her sisters-in-law, and she must make a lasting first impression. She was happy to relinquish that duty to her aunt, as she much preferred to observe her guests from afar before greeting them.

Sebastian was on a stag hunt with her father, and the pair had yet to return. She was glad the two had formed a bond; it would make it easier for her to leave when it came time to depart with her bridegroom.

She glanced down a final time before the girls disappeared into the castle. All three had blond hair, the opposite from Sebastian. Cora wondered if they had the same piercing blue eyes their brother had.

Backing away from the window, Cora turned, lifted

her skirts as she walked out of the storage room, and descended the stairs, muttering to herself as she went about how she hated being laced into a corset and forced to wear the proper fashion ladies wore. She much preferred breeches, sometimes with a shorter skirt over them. She could scarcely breathe, but she would endure for Sebastian. Soon she would become not only Sebastian's wife, but his duchess as well. Having played hostess next to her father for so many years, the idea of becoming a woman of such rank did not overwhelm her at all. She would do whatever was expected of her. All of it would be made easier knowing her husband supported her chosen profession. How it would work, she was unsure. Details still needed to be worked out.

Taking a deep breath, Cora marched out of the attic and down to greet her new sisters.

She found them all in the great hall, where her aunt was greeting them and looking as though she wasn't quite sure what to do with three exuberant young ladies.

Cora greeted the trio as she descended the last stairs. "Hello. I'm Cora."

Her aunt glared at her for being so informal. If these girls were to be part of her family, Cora refused to put on airs. She would treat them as equals—siblings.

"I'm Lady Beatrice, and these are my sisters, Lady Theodora and Lady Matilda," the tallest of the three greeted her.

Cora noted she did indeed possess the lapis blue eyes Sebastian had. All three were just as he'd described them. Tall, willowy, and quite beautiful.

"A pleasure indeed. Your brother has told me much about you."

"Speaking of our dear brother, where is he? I expected him to be here to greet us," Beatrice sniffed.

Cora knew instantly Beatrice was going to be the hardest one to accept her. "He and my father are on a stag hunt. I imagine they'll return shortly."

"They're not really going to kill one of those magnificent creatures," Matilda said.

"Don't be so silly, Matilda. Of course they are," Beatrice countered.

Theodora stood quietly, letting her sisters dominate the conversation. Sebastian had mentioned she was the quietest and most studious. Theodora seemed to use her silence to observe her sisters and what was being said around her.

"I'm sure you'd all like to rest after your journey. I'll show you to your rooms," Cora said.

"No need. One of your servants will suffice," Beatrice said.

Cora shot a look at her aunt, who was standing there stoically, trying to not reprimand the girl.

"It's no problem. I really don't mind."

She led the trio up the stairs to the guest wing. They had remained quiet, not even talking among themselves. She stopped in front of a closed oak door and opened it. "I thought you would each like your own rooms, so I had three prepared. They're all next door to each other." She walked to the next door and opened the door before repeating the gesture on the third. "I think you'll find these to your liking."

The girls followed her into the last one and watched in fascination as the two younger ones followed Beatrice's every move. "Yes, they'll do," Beatrice sniffed.

"They're really very nice," Theodora said. "I think I should like the yellow room. It's quite cheerful."

"I'll leave you to settle in. Tea is in the drawing room in an hour. Just ask one of the footmen. They'll direct you."

Cora began to leave but Beatrice spoke up.

"We'd prefer to have tea in here today."

"Verra well," Cora nodded. "I'll make sure to have it brought here. Dinner is at eight, though we gather in the drawing room at seven. I'll see you then."

She left the room without saying another word and headed back downstairs. They were indeed exactly as Sebastian had described. Lady Beatrice in particular. She was the oldest, and over time had taken on the part of being a mother figure to her two sisters, leaving Cora to wonder if perhaps that's why she hadn't married. Theodora was extraordinarily musically gifted. Matilda preferred to read and take long walks when they were in the country.

She found her aunt in the drawing room with her needlework and tea. "I see you survived."

"Yes. They're going to take tea in their rooms and rest."

"They are snotty little things, or should I say Lady Beatrice is."

Cora sat down and fixed herself a cup of tea. "Sebastian said she acted far older than her years, and that she's fiercely protective of her sisters."

"Ahhhh, that makes sense. I imagine she's been the mother figure to her younger sisters for years, and you pose an imagined threat to that hierarchy."

"Maybe once they've settled in and seen that their brother's happy, she'll settle."

"We'll see. You do have a common link you know."

"What's that, Sebastian?"

"That too, but the four of you have a bond in that

you're young and all without mothers," Henrietta said. She set her needlework aside.

"True, though Beatrice seems to be doing her best not to like me."

"That will pass once she gets to know you. Right now she's in a strange place with her sisters after a long journey. I imagine once they've seen their brother she'll settle."

"And if she doesn't?"

"Kill her with kindness, of course," Henrietta murmured, a sardonic smile on her lips.

Cora picked up her cup and thoughtfully took a sip. "Of course, but it can't be overly done. Beatrice will see right through that."

"You have to be smarter. She's going to resist anyone trying to tell her what to do, except Sebastian."

Cora smoothed her skirt down, uncomfortable with all the layers of clothing she had on. Her aunt was poring over the assortment of sweets which had been brought with tea. She chose a piece of shortbread the cook had made that morning, offering Cora one.

"Are his sisters aware of what you do?"

"I don't believe so, why?"

"Nothing. Sebastian needs to tell them. You have a race coming up. They'll wonder why you're at the stables. It's best to tell them before they find out on their own."

Cora took a bite of the delicious shortbread. "I know, and he plans to speak with them by himself. He thought it the best way to tell them."

She knew her aunt disapproved of what she did, but she paid no mind to her veiled comments.

Lady Henrietta smiled. "I commend you. As usual, you have this well planned out."

"Thank you."

Cora rose and walked over to the French doors and looked out onto the garden. Though her aunt disapproved of some of her pursuits, she was thankful she was becoming more accepting. Not having a mother of her own, she needed all the support she could find. Especially at this time with so much changing in her life. Aunt Henrietta had always been there for both her and Augustus.

SEBASTIAN MANAGED to sneak up the back stairs to his rooms without his sisters detecting him. He hadn't even stepped into the drawing room where Cora and her aunt were having tea. It wasn't that he didn't want to see them, he just knew he'd never be able to take a bath and change his clothes if his sisters discovered he'd returned from hunting. And he knew they would want him to themselves at some time, so they could riddle him with questions about Cora and what would happen once he married her.

He walked across the room and sat down. "I'm going to want to bathe before I change," he said pulling off his boots.

"I already anticipated such, Your Grace and began drawing a bath as soon as I heard you and the Duke had returned."

"Good man. Have my sisters been bothering you?"

"They made a stop when they first arrived. Beatrice wanted to be sure she knew where to find you."

"I'm sure she did," Sebastian said, with a lopsided grin.

"If you don't mind me asking, what's going to become of them once you and Lady Cora wed, Your Grace?"

"Nothing will change. Theodora will have a season, and Matilda will resume her studies at the end of the summer, and I suppose I should try and find someone Beatrice might marry. I hate the thought of her spending the rest of her life alone. They will all continue to live at Hightower Hall until they marry. Why? Did they say something?"

"No, Your Grace."

"Lady Beatrice has them all thinking otherwise." He shook his head as he rose to his full height. "She knew I would someday marry."

Titus nodded. "Yes, Your Grace, only now it's really happening."

Sebastian sighed and entered the bathing chamber. His banyan dropped to the floor and he stepped into the steaming water and sat down. He leaned against the back before submerging himself. Refreshed he wiped the water from his face and sat back to relax, knowing this would be the last time he would enjoy the quiet this day. He reached over and picked up the cloth and wintergreen soap Titus had placed on a stool next to the tub. He lathered the soap and began to wash as he wondered what sort of day Cora had had with the arrival of his sisters.

Once he finally finished and dressed, he went in search of Cora, who was reading a book near the windows. There was no sign of Aunt Henrietta.

"Fancy some tea?" she asked closing the book.

"No, my majordomo had some brought up to my rooms."

"Have you seen your sisters?"

He shook his head. "No, I came in and sneaked up the back stairs to avoid them."

She smiled. "They immediately went to their rooms when they arrived. Something about being tired from their journey and wanting to rest until you returned from hunting."

He leaned down and kissed her before sitting alongside her. "I hope Beatrice wasn't rude."

"She wasn't, though I will say she's quite overprotective of her sisters."

"That she is." He chuckled at the thought.

The couple hadn't been two minutes into their conversation when a whirlwind of skirts came bursting through the drawing room doors. How did she do it? He swore sometimes she knew he was in the house before he opened the door.

"Sebastian! When did you return?" Beatrice asked. "Why didn't you send word to us the minute you walked through the door. You know we wanted to spend time with you. Alone," She glared in their direction, though Sebastian had no doubt the stare was meant for Cora.

"Because I was tired and wanted only to bathe and change. Besides, since when did I start reporting my whereabouts to you?" He gave her a lopsided grin in an effort not to offend his sister, and that wasn't easy.

Theodora, ever the peacemaker spoke up from the chair she had sat in. "Sebastian's right. He's not a child, Beatrice."

"Would you like tea?" Cora asked.

"That would be lovely," Sebastian said. He sat against the back of the settee and waited for Beatrice's next move.

"Did you shoot a stag, Sebastian?" Matilda asked.

"Tromping about in the woods and brush to kill a defenseless deer is disgusting," Beatrice sniffed.

He ignored her remark, focusing on his other two

siblings. "No, I'm afraid he alluded us. Cora's father says he's quite good at that."

"You did see him, didn't you?" Cora asked, as she walked back to his side.

"Yes, we got a glimpse. Magnificent creature."

"He is."

"I'm so glad you didn't kill it," Theodora murmured.

"Since we have you all together, I suppose Cora and I should talk to you all about what will be happening before the wedding."

"You're really going to marry, Sebastian? Are you sure?"

He smiled at Beatrice. "Yes, I've never been so sure of anything in my life."

He glanced at Cora who was taking it all in.

"When is the wedding?" Matilda asked.

"It will be this coming Tuesday. There is a race Apollo's Gold is entered in, so we'll go cheer him on. Afterwards we'll return and we'll be married."

"When is the race?" Theodora asked.

A tray with tea had been brought in, and Cora rose to take care of serving everyone. He noted how Beatrice followed her every move.

"The race is in two days. We leave in the morning."

"Do we have to go?" Beatrice asked.

"I thought it would be a good chance for all of you to get to know Cora better."

"But we'll be seeing her all the time once you marry. We were hoping to have some time alone with you *before* you marry."

Trying to keep his temper was going to be extremely trying. Beatrice was going to be selfish, no matter what, unless it was what she wanted. He had to handle this in a calm manner, but at the same time remind his sister of who was in charge.

"I promise we'll spend an afternoon together before the wedding. Fair enough?"

Theodora and Matilda nodded in agreement, as Theodora rose and went to help Cora with the tea. Beatrice said nothing, obviously pouting. She finally nodded. "Very well, but I'm going to hold you to it, Sebastian."

He gazed over at Cora and caught her attention, noticing an amused look on her face.

"Have you girls had a chance to walk in the garden? It's really quite remarkable," he said as he accepted a cup of tea from his sister.

"No, we haven't," Matilda said.

"Let's enjoy our tea, then Cora and I can show you around," Sebastian suggested.

"That sounds delightful," Theodora said.

Beatrice was quiet, stirring her tea and ignoring everyone in the room.

~

DINNER WENT BETTER than Sebastian expected that evening. His sisters were gracious and polite to everyone, including Cora. Even Beatrice talked with Cora as the evening progressed.

After dinner, Theodora entertained everyone on piano. She was quite good. She played Mozart, who was one of her favorite composers. Theodora knew in her head every piece the man had ever written. He sat down on a nearby chair so he could observe his sisters. Cora was seated with her aunt as they all listened to the music.

~

SILENTLY HE ENTERED the darkened room. As he climbed under the covers, the mattress shifted under his weight. His mouth found hers, and he kissed her lightly on her face as she slowly woke up. Then she opened her mouth to his and he thrust his tongue into her mouth.

Desire hit him as he felt her warm hands trail over his back. He broke free of the kiss. "Take this off," He pulled at her night rail. He captured her hands and placed them above her head. He was on top of her now, and he made sure she knew who was in charge by pressing his weight down on her.

He trailed kisses along her collarbone as he pressed his cock at the top of her mound. She raised her hips and ground herself against him. He chuckled at her actions. Then his mouth found her breasts sucking one of the nipples in his mouth.

She began to shake as he settled himself between her thighs. His length pressed against her wetness as he rubbed his cock against her. He kissed her open mouth, and his weight shifted again as he drew back and found her entrance. He entered her hot, tight channel as she gasped at the sensation. He shoved again and again until he was fully seated.

Cora arched under him and gasped as he took another thrust, followed by slowly withdrawing, rubbing his flesh against her sex. He pressed his mouth slowly on hers as he felt her fly apart beneath him.

As she did, he made one or two more thrusts until his own release, as he filled her with his seed. He kissed her tenderly and released her wrists.

"So extraordinary, as always," he murmured.

She snuggled against him. "Stay? For a while?"

"Until you fall asleep."

He lay there until he felt his own eyes begin to get heavy with sleep and from being thoroughly sated. As much as he wanted to, he couldn't stay. It was too risky. Too risky he'd get caught leaving Cora's chambers.

Quickly he found his banyan, pulled it over his hard body, and padded across the room and out the door. It wouldn't be much longer before they'd be together whenever and wherever they wanted. The sooner the better, as far as he was concerned.

19

Sebastian breathed a sigh of relief as they reached their destination. Not wanting to leave his sisters alone, he brought them along, thinking seeing a horserace would give them better appreciation of why he was so passionate about the sport.

In order to get them to agree, he promised to ride with them in a separate carriage. They wanted time alone with him before he and Cora wed, and he didn't have the heart to deny any of them.

It came at a cost, as he listened to non-stop chatter the three engaged in. Everything from young men they were interested in to dresses they wanted commissioned. In the end, he was glad he'd agreed to their madness since it would probably be the last time the four of them were together as they always had been.

Cora was not spoken of, and he decided not to press the issue. They wanted their older brother to themselves and didn't want to discuss anything outside their comfort zone. Cora represented things that were changing among the four of them. It would happen again and again, until the last of his sisters married.

They followed the Duke and Augustus to the box

the family kept. Cora had walked off with her stable-master, who saw to things at the tracks when one of Cora's students raced.

"I'm going to go see that Apollo has settled in. I'll be back shortly."

Beatrice sighed. "Can't you just let others do that?"

"I won't be long," he replied, and departed the box.

He needed a short break after enduring the carriage ride with three young women. Even if they were his sisters.

He easily found his way to the track's stables and had no problem locating his stallion. He was the only horse with a woman looking on as he was readied to be saddled. Cora was speaking with a young man he immediately recognized as the jockey. He'd come to the Duke's estate to ride Apollo, and both he and Cora were satisfied he was the right fit for the stallion.

He neared the group, but as soon as Cora caught eye of him, she hurried over to his side.

"Sebastian, you must leave before Apollo sees you." She took his arm and began leading him away from the stables. He's very astute, and I'm afraid if he realizes you're nearby, he's not going to perform as well."

"You mean I'm at fault for his not-so-stellar performances?"

She nodded. "Part of the reason. The two of you share an unusual bond. Let me do it my way this time. If I'm correct he's going to race like the wind, but if he sees or even knows you're in the vicinity, all might be lost."

"Very well. We'll try it your way this time, though I shall come back after his race. Whether he wins or not."

"Thank you. I'll be along shortly."

"No, I will wait for you over by that paddock. I don't want you walking unaccompanied from the stables back to the box."

"Still don't think it's proper for a woman to be involved with horses, Your Grace?" she teased.

"You know I have no qualms about what you do. It's the way others might perceive the idea."

"And I've told you before, I don't give a fig what others think."

She lifted her skirts and returned to the group without another word. He watched as she went over final details with everyone involved.

They had been over this time and time again. He had no problem with Cora continuing with her training, though she had to understand that once they married, things might change, and as his duchess, she would have other responsibilities.

She finally joined him. "Come, let's settle in. There are two races before his."

"What do you think?" he asked, as he felt her place her hand on his forearm.

"I think he's going to bloody well blow them all away. He's ready."

"I think you're right. You've done well by him, Cora. Regardless of the outcome, you should be proud of what you've accomplished."

"He's been an easy fix and a delight to work with. I think giving him that time off was just what he needed."

"Come then, let's see how ready he is."

She smiled. "By the way, how was your journey with your sisters?"

The sides of his mouth tugged up. "Interesting. Despite their age, they still are easily amused by gowns and fripperies."

"As they should be."

"Yes, well, they'll be someone else's responsibility at some point."

"Yes," she replied with a sigh. "You do realize in two days we're to be married?"

"I've been counting every minute. I cannot wait."

"I think Augustus is a little sweet on Beatrice." She grinned as he guided her up the stairs to her father's box.

"Humph," Sebastian snorted. "Beatrice has never shown an interest in any man. Her expectations are too high. She places men on unrealistic pedestals."

"And don't you men do the same thing?"

He shook his head as they stepped inside the box. "That's different," he whispered.

Cora grinned. "Of course it is, dear."

As if to prove her point, she noticed Augustus and Beatrice together sharing a private conversation to one side of the box. Yes, her hunches were correct. Her brother had a soft spot for her. Matilda and Theodora were looking out at the racetrack below as her father pointed out spots on the track and how it all worked.

"Everything ready?" her father asked.

"Yes. It's up to Apollo now. I've done everything I can."

"When does he race, Cora?" Matilda asked, as she and her sister walked over to the table filled with food. Sandwiches, shortbread, tarts, cheese, and fruit were among the selections. She picked up a plate, still waiting for Cora's answer. Theodora cut in front of her and began choosing what fancied her.

"The next race," she replied.

Sebastian noted for the first time Cora appeared nervous. She was pacing and occasionally looking over toward the track and activity below. He wondered if it was because it was his horse, and how he did today reflected on her. She had a lot at stake with his sisters and her skeptical brother in attendance.

Whatever the outcome, he had no doubt she'd done her best. If Cora said he was ready, he was ready. There was no black-and-white when it came to the horses she trained.

~

CORA PACED THE BOX. She wanted to be with her charge, not sitting in her father's box pretending to portray the perfect, well-bred daughter of a duke.

Men and their ill-thought ideals of women. While she had been well-educated, Cora had been allowed her own interests, and developed her love of horses into a successful business. She knew as much as any of them when it came to horses, whether it be training, riding, or even breeding. Her knowledge was superior to most of the peers she knew.

She found a place to sit in the front of the box. Sebastian sat next to her, squeezing her hand. The horses were being readied and she sucked in a deep breath in nervous anticipation. She had done all she could—it was now up to Apollo's Gold.

The box was unearthly quiet as the horses broke and began to find their places. Apollo was in fourth place in the pack. Not favorable, but she knew two of the horses in front were not distance racers and would tire long before the finish.

Fists clenched, she continued to view the ongoing race from her chair. Finally, she could stand it no longer. She leapt from her chair and clung to the rail of the box, watching the colt as he passed the first contender. Cora could tell the stallion was running with his heart, his jockey urging him on.

Feeling Sebastian's presence, she quickly looked up at him before returning her attention on the evolving race below. He was as anxious as she was, his eyes never leaving the action unfolding before them.

Finally the stallion passed his next contender. The lead was now in his grasp. His rider was coaxing him on.

"Come on, come on," Cora whispered.

The race was nearing completion, and everyone was shouting now, urging the youngster along.

"Move your bloody arse!" The words escaped Cora's mouth before she could stop. She didn't dare look at anyone. Now wasn't the time.

Apollo's Gold gained on the leader and passed the bay stallion as though he were standing still. The bay was losing energy, and no matter how much his jockey urged him on, the bay did not have the stamina to re-take the lead, which so far had been his.

Leading by three lengths, Sebastian's stallion easily finished the race. He had proven he still had what it took to win.

"He did it, Cora! He did it!" Sebastian crowed, grabbing her in a hug.

"Well done, Cora," her father said.

"Why is everyone congratulating Cora?" Beatrice asked as her gaze went from her brother to Cora.

"Um, Cora's always believed he had what it took to win," Sebastian replied.

Augustus came up to Cora. "Well done. I guess you know what you're doing after all."

"Thank you. That means a lot to me, coming from you."

"Would someone please tell me what's going on here?" Beatrice wailed.

Sebastian had his hand on Cora's arm. It was time to go below for the winner. "I'll explain later."

"I'll take care of that," Augustus offered.

Sebastian nodded as he and Cora exited the box. Reaching the bottom of the stairs, he bent down. "Well done, my love."

"Apollo is the one who deserves all the credit."

"Yes, but if you hadn't believed in him like I have, he might not be here. You have a gift, Cora, a remarkable gift. I'm full of pride at what you've accomplished here today."

"Except that I can't take credit for my role in his training."

"Then I'll give you all the credit you more than deserve."

The edges of his mouth turned up into a glorious smile as he offered her his arm. She was so grateful to have found a man like Sebastian. He understood her needs and knew her most intimate thoughts and desires. He would take the praises Apollo deserved, but her hard work to get his stallion back on track had not been lost on him. She had his respect, which was more than most women got from their male counterparts.

20

Cora barely slept. Her mind would not shut off the upcoming day and all it would bring. Her wedding day. The day every young girl dreams about, though in Cora's case she had resigned herself to the fact she would probably never meet a man who would accept her the way she was. And then she met Sebastian. He was more handsome that she dared to believe she would find, and though they were at first like fire and ice, they'd managed to work through all the inconsequential matters.

She swung her legs over the side of her bed and walked over to the windows. The sun was rising. Their wedding would be blessed with one of the Highlands' most spectacular days. Outside, birds were singing and the distant trees swayed in the light breeze. She threw open one of the windows and leaned out.

Today her life would change forever. She would leave the only home she'd known to begin her new life as the Duchess of Hightower in England. It was the next chapter in the fairy tale every young girl dreams about.

Molly, her lady's maid, entered. "I have your bath ready, my lady."

"Thank you. Is everything ready?"

"Yes, my lady. You are going to be the most beautiful bride ever. You are so fortunate to have found His Grace."

"Yes, I am," she replied, turning to walk to her bathing chamber. "I only wish you were accompanying me on this next journey." Cora knew Molly was hesitant about leaving. She had family close by, and even a young man. She couldn't fault her for her decision and would find another maid once they arrived at Sebastian's home. Her home.

"Yes, my lady. I hate it, but I cannot leave my mum and da. I'm the only one living close by."

"You don't need to explain. I understand. I'll still miss you."

An hour later, seated in front of her dressing table, her maid combed her hair and elegantly fashioned it swept off her neck. Finally, after Cora's approval, a crown of flowers picked from the garden was placed on top.

She applied the faintest amount of color to her cheeks and lips and nodded. As she began to stand, Aunt Henrietta walked in. She was dressed in an elegant, dark-blue muslin dress.

"I just came to wish you well, and to answer any questions you might have," she said. "Though I doubt you have any." She cackled and kissed Cora on the cheek.

"Thank you, Auntie. You have been such a guiding force for me since Mother died. I have to give you a lot of credit for that."

She saw her aunt wipe tears of joy from her eyes.

"Come on, let's get you dressed. Your duke is waiting."

"Patiently I hope."

"He's going to be at a loss for words the moment you walk in the room."

Her maid began to help her into the ivory satin gown. Dainty seed pearl buttons ran up the front of the bodice. The bustle and train were modest, as Cora hated having so much fabric behind her. Her father had given her pearls which belonged to her mother as a gift. The three strands fit perfectly and complimented the dress. Cora touched the pearls with her hand. What she would give to have her mother here today on this joyful occasion!

Finally, her aunt and maid deemed her ready to make the short walk to the family chapel. She walked down the staircase for the final time as an unmarried young woman. Her aunt followed, and together they stepped outside and walked the path leading to the chapel.

As she entered the chapel, her eyes immediately found Sebastian standing at the altar with the priest and Allgood. He stood tall, wearing a dark gray suit with a crisp white shirt. So handsome, so masculine. Their eyes met and those luscious lips of his formed a lopsided grin of approval.

He'd asked his close friend Allgood if he'd do the honor of standing up with him. Crispin graciously agreed, happy his friend had at last found happiness.

Her father came to her side and together they walked down the short aisle. She passed her aunt and Sebastian's three sisters, all of whom were smiling.

A moment later, the Duke was handing her over to Sebastian. He kissed her on the cheek and smiled at her. She knew he was wishing her mother were here as well. His face gave away his most private emotions. Especially when it came to his late duchess.

Her hands were shaking as she took Sebastian's

hand. He smiled down at her as he covered her hand with his other, as they turned to face the priest.

Cora repeated her vows to Sebastian, a sense of calm enveloping her as she did. She listened to him say his vows, again his eyes never leaving hers. As he finished, he placed a gold band on her finger, and just that quick, they were husband and wife.

He leaned down and kissed her, probably longer than he should have, but neither of them cared. A sound of the priest clearing his throat brought them back to reality. They greeted their guests, then followed the priest to the back of the kirk and signed the register.

They were met by their guests with red rose petals as they walked out of the kirk. Everyone walked together, Cora holding on tightly to Sebastian's arm. As they neared the castle entrance they were greeted by her father's staff, who roared their approval.

His heart skipped a beat the moment she entered the kirk on the arm of her father. She was perfection of what a bride should look like, dressed in a gown with a crown of flowers atop her hair. He couldn't take his eyes off her elegant long neck bathed in a triple strand of pearls. He shed any thoughts of kissing her from head to toe, naked except for her necklace. He would give her jewels, lots of them, and yes, there would be much love-making wearing just her jewelry. She was the most beautiful woman in the world and took his breath away.

As her father handed her off to him, he caught the familiar scent of oranges and vanilla. Immediately he felt himself relax.

The rest of the ceremony was a blur. As she repeated her vows to him, he noted a pink had risen in her cheeks. In spite of her sudden shyness, she repeated her vows without hesitation. When she finished, she peered into his eyes and gave him a knowing smile.

He had promised to love her in every possible way. He would give her the moon if it were possible. Never had he had such strong emotions for another. Cora brought out the best in him, and he vowed he would never falter. She was the most important thing in his life. His wife, his duchess.

Finally, after vows were said and the priest had pronounced them husband and wife, Sebastian held her face in his hands and kissed her thoroughly. In front of family and all. She was now his wife, and he wanted there to be no doubt of his love for this remarkable woman. Their lives would now be intertwined forever.

PREVIEW: THE MAKING OF A DUKE

LOVE AND DEVOTION / BOOK 4

PROLOGUE

The last place Augustus Keats, the Marquess of Talisker, wanted to be this evening was a ball. He'd just arrived from his home in Scotland and had much business to attend to, but let his long-time friend Lord Edward Findley convince him he needed to attend, if for no other reason, it would let people know he'd returned.

His life had been in tatters for over a year, and recovery difficult. Flippant ways led to him owing to friends, now former friends, a ridiculously vast sum of money from his gambling. His brother-in-law, The Duke of Hightower, lent him the money to pay off his debts, but that had come at a cost. Hightower, at least for the immediate future, held an interest in the family whiskey distillery. The agreement made with his father left Augustus with a slim share of the profits.

Unwilling to live off the meager amount and finding him forced out of the day-to-day operations, he started his own distillery with a generous loan from his aunt. His first two batches were aging and wouldn't be ready for at least two years. He readied for a third bottling, and in the meantime, he found himself forced to live off his estate's earnings, money left over from his aunt's money, and the pittance of his father's whiskey business.

Findley suggested he find a bride. One with a generous dowry. Not that he hadn't thought of that before. That would take care of a lot of his immediate problems—a marriage of convenience. After his wife bore him a couple of sons, he could set her up elsewhere, and he wouldn't have to set eyes on her.

As the heir to a dukedom, life had never been an easy road for Augustus. He and his father shared little in common, which, until recent years, hadn't caused a problem. They worked around it. Now a rift had grown between them, and he blamed his sister and her husband for making things worse.

Glancing across the ballroom, he saw her. Lady Beatrice Steele, older sister of his brother-in-law. Beatrice was even more attractive than the last time he'd seen her. She was tall, willowy, and her figure curved like an hourglass, in all the right places, and stunning, as he remembered.

The pair became friends while she and her sisters visited for their brother's wedding in Scotland, and he found himself attracted to her. She was bold and opinionated, much like his sister Cora, but unlike his sister, Lady Beatrice knew where boundaries lay.

Though he tried to further their friendship, Lady Beatrice made it known she wasn't interested. She put her own future on hold until her two younger sisters were settled.

Their eyes locked, and she flashed him a seductive grin before turning and making her way to the French doors leading out to the gardens. What was she up to, going outside alone and unescorted? There were always one or two rakes who bided their time waiting for someone like Lady Beatrice whom they could easily take advantage of.

She looked seductively over her shoulder at him one last time before disappearing.

Intrigued and worried for her safety, Augustus hurried across the room and out the French doors. She was nowhere to be seen.

He ventured out into the gardens, the pathways lit by torches, until he found her. She was sitting on a wooden bench in front of a pond the Countess of Mulberry was famous for. The Countess had seen one similar on a journey she and her husband made to the Far East, and immediately upon their return had one installed in both their London home and their country estate. Or so the story went.

Upon seeing him approach, she rose from the wooden bench. Her golden hair sparkled in the moonlight. She looked like a goddess in a dark-blue silk confection that hugged her luscious curves in all the right places.

Augustus approached without saying a word. This time, she would remember exactly who he was. Taking her arm with one hand, he cupped her face with the other and boldly kissed her. Lost in his lust and need for her, he parted her lips with his tongue. She seemed to enjoy his advances, opening to him. Perhaps a little too easily.

The next thing he remembered was Lady Beatrice pulling back, ending the kiss, and slapping him as hard as she could across his face before pushing him into the Countess's pond.

"What was that for?" he sputtered. He landed on his backside, not an inch of him left dry. Looking through wet hair now plastered to his face, he saw her backside as she hurried off without a glance.

Augustus threw his head back and began laughing, his rumbling baritone echoing throughout the gardens. Wiping his face with his hands, he pushed wet hair out of his eyes. The minx! What had he done to deserve such a greeting? Whatever it was, his interest was now piqued. He could play her game of cat-and-mouse for as long as she wanted. Sooner or later, she would tire, and he'd capture her.

ALSO BY JR SALISBURY

MAYFAIR

Dealing with the Duchess

Ravaging the Duke

To Love An Earl

The Marquess Takes A Bride

MACLEODS OF SKYE

Donnan's Rose

The Sins of Rory MacLeod

Lord Malcolm's Heart

Taming Lily

The Wicked Seduction of Wallace MacLeod

LOVE AND DEVOTION

Wish Upon A Duke

Once Upon A Countess

Seduction of a Duke

Second Chance At Love

ABOUT THE AUTHOR

J. R. Salisbury is the historical romance alter-ego of contemporary romance author Jamie Salisbury. Writing romance stories with passion and sass, Jamie Salisbury has seen several of her books soar to #1 on Amazon. Her novella, Tudor Rubato was a finalist in the 2012 RONE awards. The cover won for Best Contemporary Cover. In 2014, her novel, Life and Lies was nominated for a RONE in the Erotica category.

Music, traveling and history are among her passions when not writing. Her previous career in public relations in and around the entertainment field has afforded her with a treasure trove of endless story ideas.

Follow Jamie:
Book + Main
Website